JOURNEYS FROM A BOY TO A MAN

by

Linda L. Lattimer

WHISKEY CREEK PRESS
www.whiskeycreekpress.com

Published by
WHISKEY CREEK PRESS

Whiskey Creek Press
PO Box 51052
Casper, WY 82605-1052
www.whiskeycreekpress.com

ISBN 1-59374-543-5

Credits
Cover Artist: Jinger Heaston
Editor: Marsha Briscoe

Printed in the United States of America

Dedication

~~Always to God above~~

~~To Bob's long lost sister, Marvetta. The last time he saw her, he was ten-years-old; she was only three when their mother died. He never saw her again and was never able to locate her.~~

~~To Bob's brothers: Larry, Dick, Jim, and Curtis (John died in a car accident)~~

~~To Bob's Aunt and Uncle who helped raise him after his mother's death and the family split. (In loving memory to Uncle Gerald who died this past June)~~

~~To *all* the Beasley family who showed me much love when I visited them, and when they came to visit me. I miss Aunt Bessie's ghost stories, Aunt Shirley's laughter, Aunt Inez's cakes and great food. To a mother-in-law that I got along with and a father-in-law with whom I was always able to share talks~~

~~To Bob's father-in-law: In loving memory of Top, (Ray Boggs) "He was like the father I never had. I really enjoyed our talks. I missed you when you lost your battle with cancer on May 2, 1991."~~

~~To three beautiful daughters that any parent would be proud to love. Marvetta, Suzanne and Lisa Reneé (Bob and Linda's lovely daughters), I love you much. I am glad I was there to see you get married and give me three wonderful sons-in-law, Richard, TR and Tommy, and four great grandsons, Allen, Robert, Dylan and Dakota~~

~~To a marriage that withstood time, no matter what the odds. *The deck was full and we came out winning. Just wish we could have had more time together.*~~

~~And in loving memory of Robert (Bob) M. Lattimer— May 26, 2005. *My journey has ended. I lost my battle, too.*~~

~~To Dolly Parton who granted my last wish to see her before the cancer totally consumed my body. "You treated me like family and I never forgot your kindness." Thank you to all the people at Dollywood for that day, and special thanks to Karen Wilson for the invitation.~~

~~And to all the Veterans who served and serve our country proudly...sometimes they are sadly forgotten. But their journeys still remain.~~

~~All the above dedication is what Bob had wanted in the book if it were ever published. Many of his family would call him 'Mike.'~~

~~To all the Beasley family who showed me much love when I visited them, and when they came to visit me. I miss Aunt Bessie's ghost stories, Aunt Shirley's laughter, Aunt Inez's cakes and great food. (We lost Uncle Woodrow Beasley, December 19, 2004, and miss him dearly) To a mother-in-law that I got along with and a father-in-law with whom I was always able to share talks~~

ACKNOWLEDGMENTS

I would like to especially thank Marsha Briscoe for all her help in the editing of this book. And a very special thanks to Debra Womack and Whiskey Creek Press. And to Jinger Heaston for the beautiful cover.

Also a special thanks to Dr. Deborah Daniels and her wonderful staff, Regina and Denise and Kathy, who were very caring and helpful to Bob. He always spoke highly of Dr. Daniels.

Thanks to all the friendly people at John B. Amos Cancer Center, Melinda, Starla, Cheryl and all the other nurses and assistants who took special care of Bob during his chemo and radiation treatments. Your friendly smiles and soothing conversation helped to ease some of his pain.

Thanks to Ruby Smith and her family for all their love and prayers.

Thanks to Sue Vetter for her kindness and help during this time.

And to Woody and Susan Weaver, a great brother and sister-in-law and their girls, Melissa and Melanie...thanks for all the laughs and good times we were able to share.

Contents:

Ticket Anyone?
Introduction

I suppose if man were to compose his thoughts, his journeys from the day he was born to the day of his death, he would undoubtedly have many travels to tell and some to even boast of. His conquests, his adventures, misadventures, love life, love affairs—the list would run forever, and no matter what man wrote concerning his saga, or his tall tale, every word that he put in that manuscript would be different than the next. For throughout one's life, no two stories could ever be the same or carry such potential value as those of the man who has lived his own story. Each story would have a unique beginning and untimely ending. Those fortunate to be born indeed have to face, at some point, death. There is no escaping and no place to run and hide once a man's number has been called.

While birth begins man's traveling days; the ticket that is handed out can only be used for the time he has scheduled to spend on earth. The choices should be wise in everything that he sets out to accomplish. With his days, he has laughter, pain, sorrow, and any emotion that he might encounter in his travels. There are loves found and loves lost. But whatever journey man happens upon, it is sure to be a book, in a shell of its own.

The Arrival
Mike's Entry

It was late in the month of March when he pushed his way into this world. Of course he had no choice in what month to actually arrive; all he knew was the time of his entering was nigh. There was a kick, a small jab and bingo—the pain, the contraction, was inflicted and felt. Within minutes he would be sliding down the narrow passageway, finally meeting the one person who had been catering to his needs. The atmosphere would be entirely different than the one he had been accustomed to the last nine months. In his tiny world he had been safe and free from all the pollution that society had placed upon the world. Little did he know the New World he was entering would be so different from his last home. He would soon find himself encountering new and exciting adventures.

There was a light, and then many lights, as he came slipping out the canal opening. Oops, was he going to fall? No, there was a warm hand on the end grasping hold of his wet, sticky, red body. He remembered being held by his two feet as the man wearing glasses whacked his buttocks. A sharp, squealing sound issued from his lips. A cry, he found out later, they called it. Something that many newborns, as well as others, did a lot.

Some used its source to get away with anything, while others needed it to express trouble or pain. Maybe this place wasn't going to be so bad after all, his little mind reasoned.

He was handed to a woman in white. He learned later that she was called a nurse. She began cleaning his soiled body. He was a mess; that was for sure. As she wiped each part of his body, he observed the red stain quickly vanish to be replaced by white. This procedure was strange, but he figured it was part of his new life.

Finally, after his rinsing, the nurse wrapped him in a tiny blanket. It was a good thing, too. His tiny body was beginning to get a chill. It may have been the end of March but for the town of Logan, Ohio, there was still a snip of coldness in the valley. He longed to be back in his little round shell; at least it had been warm and cozy.

He was handed to another woman lying in a bed. He soon discovered the beautiful black haired woman, with the hazel green eyes and loveliest smile to warm any man's heart, was his mother. Her skin was fair and the touch of her hand was soft beyond compare. It was here that he began feeling safe and snug once again, with no threat to his existence. Truly this moment was better than the nourishment he had been receiving in the tiny compartment before emerging into this New World.

Just when he thought he was going to have total undivided attention, a tall, slim man with lines running through his forehead, and a tiny brush of hair growing across his top lip, entered the room. He quickly discovered this man was his father. Now there would be three of them to share fun happy times together.

But wait, who was walking into the room now? His tiny

eyes looked over toward the doorway. There stood a tall, skinny boy with jet-black hair. Next to him was another boy, a few inches less in height, but carrying a few more pounds than the first on his frame. The third was slightly shorter than the two but very thin. His little ears seem to be protruding. There was no mistaking the resemblance; each was related to the mother and father. His thought of being alone with only one person to share this blissful moment soon disappeared. He found out he had what others termed *a family*.

Well, no sense in backing out now. There was no way he could return to where he just left. Only one thing remained to do. With all his might he bellowed out the loudest cry that he could muster. In no time, father and brothers departed the room, leaving mother to nurse her newborn son. Yeah, he had discovered power in this newfound weapon of the cry.

The Trademark
Mike's Dilemma

The month of April sent many showers along the border of Ohio. Many would comment that the rain would bring beautiful May flowers. Days rapidly flashed before the young boy's eyes as he found his body stretching with each passing day. His tiny hands and feet were growing and his frame was also expanding. Still, his brothers called him *the runt*. Scrawny *little Mike,* they would chant.

"Boys, leave your brother alone," Mother would insist. "You should remember at one time you were tiny and new, too. Now stop pestering your brother and run off and play."

It didn't matter how often his mother would instruct the other brothers to leave him alone, they would continue to call him *the runt* and make funny, weird faces at the little fella. That was all right though, Mike thought, as he watched them from a distance. His day would come and he would be sure to get them for all the little annoyances they inflicted on him. *Just you wait,* he mumbled under his breath, in goo baby talk. *I'll get you all.*

The days soon developed into months, and months into years, as little Mike's body began growing from infant to young boy. The stages of his growth were exciting as he observed all the changes in his anatomy. No wonder his first home could no longer house him after those first nine months. The tiny woman who had given him birth would have been unable to contain so much sprouting of another human.

Later he witnessed his mother's small body grow larger in the area of her stomach, and with each time, three other infants were dropped into their home. No longer was he the baby of the family. Two of the times, there had been two additional boys, each bearing a strong resemblance to the other family members. In all the boys, their ears were what stood out in the crowd. As Mike eyed his in the mirror, he realized his were the ones that stuck out the most.

"Oh, no," he muttered as he continued to stare at his ears.

Was he destined to be the butt of the jokes with all the other children? If his brothers called him *the runt,* imagine what others would hasten to call him once they saw his ears. No, this could never happen. Something had to be done.

He went to the only person who would listen—his mother.

"Mike, honey, there is nothing wrong with your ears. I don't want you to listen to others. As you grow older, you will learn that life can be unfair. People can be really cruel and use words to inflict pain. I don't want you paying any attention to jokers. Promise me?"

He lowered his head in disappointment. "Yes, Mother."

She saw the sad look displayed on her son's face. At the moment there was no cure to administer. Protruding ears had always been the trademark of their family. With her stretched out arms, she invited him to enter, to be caressed and held with a motherly hug. He responded earnestly. There had been less time for these moments since the birth of the other children.

As time progressed, Mike was plagued with name-calling by others who saw him. The favorites of the school children ran the gamut of a *taxi cab with its doors open,* to *big ears,* to *with ears the size of donuts,* he really should have no problem in hearing.

The toll on the young boy was mounting. He didn't know how much longer he would be able to tolerate the children's stares, let alone the brutality of their cold words. Both parents sensed his pain and worried that the insults from other children might diminish any fun the young boy should have been enjoying. Instead of experiencing happy days, his days were filled with tears from the insults he had to endure.

After a month of Mike's continuous crying, his father decided to take him to a doctor. His first visit was enough to bring a sunny glow to Mike's face. There was an alternative. Since the large ears were already causing some difficulty, the doctor suggested something similar to plastic surgery.

They could be pinned back and reconstructed for better shaping, according to the doctor. Being a coal miner, Mike's father wondered if the family could afford an operation. He also knew what it would do for his son's self-esteem. The doctor assured them the price would be in a range that would not destroy their finances. It would be a surgery well worth its money and would benefit Mike in the long run. The parents agreed to the procedure.

After the surgery, Mike's ears were very tender. The doctor said it would take a few days before the soreness left. But the soreness did pave the way for Mike to receive much loving attention from his mother until he fully mended, something that he had missed with the new additions in the family. It felt good all over to again be the center of attention, for a while, amidst all the other siblings.

It didn't take long for his ears to mend. They still were not small ears. The only difference was they no longer stuck out. That alone was more than enough to make Mike's life happy. He was still deemed *the runt* of the family but no longer did anyone make fun of his ears. It was a time that he once again was feeling that warm security-blanket-closeness he shared with his dear mother when he first entered the cold world.

Absolutely No Females Allowed!
The Sister

Ever notice how a family can grow after a child is born? It seemed like no sooner than one sibling had entered, making a mark on the world, than Mike's mother and father were telling him another one was soon to be delivered. Boy, what a let down. He was finally getting some of the things he wanted in life, and bingo, his mother was having another baby. Before he knew what was happening, nine months had passed and his mother was bringing the bundle home.

They waited in anticipation for the next male to be shown to them. But something happened, someone steered the wrong course...it wasn't a boy.

A *girl* was what they were informed. "You have a baby sister."

They eyed each other in morbid fright. "Oh, no." The loud moan swirled through the air. "Send it back to the hospital." What were their parents thinking? This was an all-male family, with the exception of their mother. No way could another female be accepted into the family. But she would not be returned. She was here to stay. That was all that had to be said on the matter.

Ironic how *she* ended up getting all the attention. At least that was what all the brothers thought. Was it because she was the last or because she was different from the rest? Whatever the reason, after they allowed themselves to grow close to her, they were a complete family with both sexes of children. Nothing, and no one, could ever separate the happiness they continued to share with each passing day.

The times were hard, money scarce. But Mike's parents made sure that none of them ever lacked the necessities of life. This young female who had brought joy to the males and had bonded with them had indeed captured their hearts.

They soon learned that little sister, as well as any other female who happened into their circle, would prove a big help to their mother.

As Mike settled in the great big armchair and stretched out his tiny legs, a thought occurred to him: if his mother would only have a greater supply of girls than boys, the men would have it made. They could just kick back and allow the females to cater to their every whim. Something told him that from now on, any female would be cordially welcomed into their all male world. A huge grin stretched his lips. What a wonderful life that would be for the menfolk in the family.

Teacher's Pet
A Lesson Learned the Hard Way

There are many faces that stick in people's minds as they go through life. There are some good, some wonderful, and some many would rather forget. Growing up and going to school, children normally have a friend that they hate to part with when they become older. If not a friend, a girl that steals their heart or a teacher that remains embedded within the mind. Mike had one teacher in the first grade that he would never forget.

There was a little short girl with red pigtails, who wore glasses and sat behind him. She loved to pester and harass him continuously, day in and day out. She would jab him in the back of his head or poke him on the shoulder with the tip of her pencil, anything that would annoy him and try his patience. It was becoming a struggle of wits with her everyday. One day she went too far and Mike could no longer maintain his composure. Without thinking, Mike looked directly into her face and called her a name that his mother would not think too highly of her son rolling off his tongue. He called her *ugly four eyes, piggy tail shorty.*

In no time the teacher was standing behind him, with her right hand clasped on his shoulder. She instructed Mike to follow her to the front of the class. Worried, he swallowed hard. He knew what she had in store for him. She reached for the wood paddle that hung in front of her desk, the one that confronted students as they entered each morning, the one that seemed to say, *come on kids, let me warm your little behinds today. Give the teacher a hard time, so I can be useful instead of hanging around, gathering dust.*

When Mike tried to explain the situation, she refused to listen. She had heard what he called the girl and it was not proper to go around calling a young girl names. He had been caught red-handed, so to speak. When he tried once more to tell her how Mary Ann had pestered him, the teacher only shook her head in disbelief. Instead, she chose to accept Mary Ann Tasmor's story, which was a bold face pack of lies.

Miss Willard wasn't exactly the kind of teacher you fell in love with. She was sort of matronly. Many of the students would kid about her sagging bosoms and thick thunder legs. If she happened to overhear their remarks, she would give those students bad grades, stating they had the devil in them. This was Mike's first full-fledged encounter with her. He wasn't looking forward to that wood paddle being applied to his bottom.

At the time, he didn't know why she was asking what date his birthday fell on. If he had known, he would have said the first, and not the twenty-sixth. Miss Willard took the wood paddle and whacked his bottom twenty-six times before she decided to call it quits. Whacked him right in front of the whole class as they watched in awe. Mary Ann sat smiling the whole time.

After she finished the last strike, Mike didn't stay around for the class to see him cry. With every ounce of power he had in his small legs, he hurriedly ran home. He needed to see his mother. Most importantly, he really needed a hug.

She was standing at the ironing board pressing a shirt when he entered the door. One look at his red-beet face, with tears streaming from his eyes, and she instantly forgot all about any ironing. She ran over to see what was wrong. Had he been in a fight? Was he hurt? Sick? What?

Slowly Mike forced the words from his mouth. His mother was very sympathetic, but she soon was angry at the teacher's behavior. She went into the bathroom and wet a face cloth to clean his little face. When she embraced him warmly with another hug, he felt relieved by her kindness. It was like all his pain had vanished for a moment.

She unplugged the iron and moved it to another surface before she left the house. She had words to say to that teacher. She told Mike to stay put until she returned. After she exited the door, he ran to his bedroom, flung himself across the bed, and cried tears of pain. His bottom was very sore and it hurt badly. He wondered how long that pain would last, and if he would even be able to sit in the desk at school without feeling a good deal of discomfort.

That night Mike overheard his mother and father talking about Miss Willard. Mike's father was proud of the way his wife had handled the matter. Not many mothers would have confronted *the ole battle-axe* as some referred her. He didn't think the woman had any right hitting his child twenty-six times. He made a point to see the principal the next day over the matter. It was hard taking time off from work for such matters when he had so many mouths to feed, but that policy should never have been invoked on a child.

Mike's butt continued to stay sore for at least a week, but

the pain was all but forgotten with each passing day. Miss Willard was another story. Years later he still remembered her discipline. Once thing was certain, Mrs. Willard never once punished a child in that manner again. As for Mary Ann, she was moved behind another boy and was no longer Mike's problem.

The Bed Wetter
Hiding Secrets

As a parent, sometimes one finds that the most difficult task in teaching children is the self-control of getting up and going to the bathroom without wetting themselves or the bed. Yes, potty training was one technique that truly fascinated Mike as he observed his father being a dad. It could be a nuisance but it could also, on the other hand, be richly rewarding if the child would heed the parent's words, or perhaps the parent's encouragement.

Mike had a small problem of bed-wetting when he was younger, something his father quickly, upon discovery, put a stop to. Mike thought, after his brief encounter with the young girl in school, that there would be no more problems in his life. Boy was he wrong. After supper, he would love to drink tons and tons of water. He knew that he couldn't hold an exact ton, but for a small child that choice of word suited the occasion. The only problem about drinking so much at night was having to get out of a comfortable bed to go to the bathroom.

It seemed his kidneys were having a fun time calling the bladder to hurry and get to the toilet. One night when they summoned for immediate draining, he was just too tired to move. Or perhaps too lazy, he never could fathom which. Soon he felt the warm urine ooze out, dampening the sheets beneath him. Too tired and sleepy to move, he lay there until morning.

When the sun's rays broke through the curtains, he quickly jumped out of the bed. The sheets no longer felt wet. With that in mind, he threw the covers onto the bed. Mother would surely be impressed with these actions. Also it was a good way not to get caught.

This went on for about a week until one bright morning his father happened into the room. The smell of the urine was starting to make its way up through the lining of the mattress. His daddy walked in and sniffed the area.

He leaned tall over Mike, shadowing him with a stern gaze. "Son, have you been wetting your bed?"

Afraid, Mike didn't say a word.

His dad gave the boy one lingering glance then walked over to the bed. With one hand his daddy pulled the covers down. The sheets were soiled and the stench was awful.

"No wonder you didn't want your mother to make your bed. I am really shocked with you, *son*."

Oh no, there was that one word alone that made you feel uncomfortable. He had a habit of referring to any of the boys as *son* when he was not happy with their behavior.

Mike continued standing, eyeing his every move. He felt cornered like a rat, with no place to run.

"Son, this has to stop."

"I'm sorry, Daddy. It won't happen again. It was only one time," Mike lied as his gaze lowered to the floor. His words were choppy.

"Only one time? Are you sure, son? We taught you children never to lie."

Mike eyed his dad then shifted his gaze to the floor once more.

"Are you sure, son?"

Mike stood speechless as he once again met his dad's stare.

His dad drew in a breath, then motioned for Mike to come over to the bed. Mike slowly edged his way toward him. As long as he lived, he would never forget what his daddy did next. He grabbed hold of Mike's head and buried his nose and face deep into the soiled sheets. The foul odor of the urine was enough to make him vomit, but he didn't dare.

"I don't think you will lie to me again, *son*, when I ask for a direct answer."

Mike never understood if his dad did it because he was not being truthful or for wetting the bed. After the incident of having his nose rubbed into the terrible stench, one thing happened; he no longer wet the bed. He wasn't sure that his daddy's procedure was appropriate for another child, but it was one he never tried on any of his children.

The Girl Next Door
Orange Crush

One thing about having many children in a family is that there was always someone to play with or share time with. There was always someone to play tag or throw the ball to. But there comes a time when you seek more than a family member. You seek a close friend.

Walter and Mike seemed to be the ones who were always together. They shared secrets that only friends shared. They hated to have their territory invaded by anyone, especially the freckled face girl next door. She had a loud mouth and was constantly running telling her mother everything Walter and Mike did. Living next door to Walter's house, she insisted upon peering through the bushes to see what they were doing every time they got together outside.

As they sat in the backyard sipping Orange Crush drinks, she stuck her head into their midst.

"Hey, what are you two doing?" she asked in her silly little voice.

"Nothing," Walter remarked.

"You must be doing something." She giggled. "Can I come over?"

"No! Go on and play with your dolls," Walter said.

"Got anymore of that orange drink?" she quizzed while licking her lips.

"Don't think so."

Walter was really great on words. He always resented the girl entering his domain. He kept his cool, his eyes focused past the girl as he stared at the bushes.

"Can I have some of yours, Walter?"

His gaze quickly moved toward her. Was she never going to leave? Couldn't she get the hint? He cast a hateful stare into her path.

"Didn't I tell you to run along home and play with your dolls? Leave us men alone."

She folded her arms over her chest. "You aren't men! You're little boys."

That didn't set too well with Walter who would have preferred her to be a boy about that time so he could have knocked the block off her shoulder. He gave her another little glance, then slowly took another tiny sip of the Orange Crush drink.

She continued eyeing them as they sipped away at the drinks. The saliva was practically dripping from her tongue as she yearned for a taste of that drink. Mike could almost imagine what she was going through. It was a miracle when they were given a soda of any kind. With so many children in the house, they seldom received such luxuries.

When their mother was able to get them an Orange Crush, it was like a gift to each of them, something that they thoroughly enjoyed. With money being scarce, and so many children in the household, an Orange Crush was like—*Wow!*

It was hard enough having to share with siblings. He could understand why he didn't wish to share with the girl next door. Not when she was the only child in the family and was better off than they were. Anyone in the neighborhood could tell you that.

Walter's family was the same. They had four children, but his mother had been kind enough to give both of them a whole drink today. Since Mike had helped Walter with taking the garbage out and picking up around in the yard, Walter's mother had rewarded them both.

She raised her eyebrow and gave them a devilish grin. "If you don't give me some of your drink, I'm going to run and tell my mother then she will tell your mother. I will make sure you both get a harsh whipping."

Walter looked at the ground while he sketched his finger around in the sand.

"Hey, we don't have much left in our bottles. Go tell your mother to get you some at the store. We have a lot more children in our family that we have to share with."

"NO!" she shouted. "I demand to have some of yours…now! You gave Mike some. You can give me some, too, *Walter.*" She leaned over with hands flattened on her hips.

Walter jumped up from the ground and cast an evil look in her direction. "Don't you have someone else to go pester?"

"Not until I have some of that Orange Crush drink!"

He rubbed a hand over his thigh. "I guess I can go see if there are any left in the refrigerator."

She smiled and hummed as Walter went into the house. When he returned, his bottle was half full.

"Here, you can have some of mine. There ain't no more in the refrigerator." He extended his hand to give her the drink.

"*Ain't* isn't a word. You need to be listening in school." Hastily she snatched it from him and put the bottle to her lips. Turning it upside down, she drank it, looked at him, then drank some more.

"Sorry, Walter, I drank it all," she said as she tossed the bottle down at his feet. "Na, ne, ne, na, na," she taunted and laughed, then ran to her house.

For the life of him, Mike didn't understand where Walter had gotten more orange pop. Walter's mother had given them the last two bottles. When he went in the house, his bottle was practically empty. Mike questioned him about the matter and he burst out in laughter.

"It weren't no orange drink. I had to pee, so I used the bottle." Walter smirked.

Mike's mouth flew open as if to catch a fly. He couldn't believe his ears.

"Walter, you didn't. Tell me you didn't."

"Look, she asked for it. She's nothing but a constant badger, always sticking her nose where it don't belong. I am really growing weary of her living next door. Every time we turn around, she's there. Don't tell me you enjoy her company."

Mike shook his head no. He was right. She was a bother.

"If you tell anyone, you know our parents will tan our behinds, besides I will deny it."

No, there wasn't any way he would tell anyone of this little episode. He would be just as guilty as Walter, he would see to that. They kept that little secret to themselves; one of many that Mike ended up sharing with his best friend.

The little girl whom Walter had termed as *the enemy* never crossed over into their territory again. They made sure about that. He and Walter sought other places to play or relax, with absolutely no interruptions of any kind.

Can She Bake A Cherry Pie!
The Lie

When people looked at a cherry tree or bit into a piece of cherry pie, Mike wondered if they ever recalled the story of George Washington and the incident of the cherry tree. He was quoted as saying, "I cannot tell a lie. I did it with my little hatchet."

Whether or not Mason Locke Weem's book, *The Life and Memorable Actions of George Washington,* was indeed accurate, it was what that one segment said about the first president that Mike would always call to mind. Many insisted it to be true, while others replied otherwise. For Mike and his account about the incident of the cherry pie, he knew it was true. It was one story that rang clearly, even in his older years.

His mother could cook, really cook. Her baking was better than anyone's. Whenever she made any cookies, pies or cakes, they didn't linger for long in their home. All of her brood made sure of that.

It was a sunny, warm day in July when his mother placed the freshly baked pie on the window sill, before she and the others left early to go shopping. Mike was alone in the house with the cherry pie, at least he thought he was. He should have known that his mother would never really leave him alone to go shopping. The aroma was drawing him closer to it, almost like a hypnotic trance. He went straight to the windowsill and admired the pie as the steam slowly eased from the crust.

Standing on his tiptoes, he took a finger and thrust it deep into the center of the pie, then licked the sweet nectar off his finger. The mere taste was better than anything he could ever dream. As he stood licking the evidence from his finger, he wasn't aware his father was standing in the hallway observing his every move. With the last tiny fragment removed from his little finger, he turned and saw his father.

Mike swallowed hard enough to be heard even down the street. Oops, had he seen what he had done? Surely not. Besides there was no proof. His finger was clean as a whistle. His father walked over toward him and gazed at the pie. An impression had been made in the crust.

"Mike, did you stick your finger in your mother's fresh baked cherry pie?" His father's voice was bold, stern. His body towered over Mike as he looked down at his son's short thin frame.

"Who me?" Mike asked, surprised, trying not to show any sign of guilt. "No, Daddy, I was just looking at it."

"You sure about that, *son?*"

Oh no, there was that *son* remark. Mike nodded to let him know he was more than sure. He even stuck out his finger allowing him to see no stain of cherry pie had even touched its surface.

"You could ask Billy. He is always messing with things he isn't supposed to." Really great, Mike, blame your younger brother. Dig the hole to your grave a little deeper. "I can't even reach the pie, see?" he said while reaching with his hand.

"Son, you know one thing I cannot tolerate is for someone to lie to me."

"Yes, sir."

"All you would have to do is stand on your tip toes. Or get a chair. Now did you stick your finger in the pie?"

What was wrong with the man today? Wasn't his answer sufficient? It wasn't like he had eyes all over and could see his every move.

"Are you going to tell me the truth?"

"No, Daddy, it wasn't me," he lied in an innocent tone.

His eyes grew large, as the veins in his neck began to pop out. He was, without a doubt, very upset with Mike.

"Mike, I am not punishing you for sticking your finger in the cherry pie, but for the lie you just told me." He pointed over toward the hallway. "I was standing right over there when I saw you stick your finger in the pie. You deliberately stood there and told me a bold face lie, Mike. Now, I will ask you once more, before I spank your little rear. Did you do it?"

For the life of him, Mike still could not fess up. Here the man had seen the whole thing, caught him in the act, and he couldn't tell him the truth. With all the boldness he could muster, he looked deep into his father's eyes and answered his question.

"No, Daddy."

Nothing more was said. He took hold of Mike and gave him a whipping. Mike later wondered if he had told him the truth, would his father have let it go? But he knew his fear of actually confessing the truth weighed heavy on him. It was a lesson, on a bright, sunny morning in July that he knew he would always call to remembrance, especially whenever he bit into a piece of cherry pie. That was the last time he ever lied to his father.

Man's Best Friend
Bridget

The sign read: *Welcome FFA, Future Farmers of America*. He browsed through all the brochures and pamphlets that lay on the table in front of him, and considered what a joy it would be to join such a function. If anything, maybe he would get lucky and get out of doing any chores around the house. Yeah, that would be great. Just explain to his parents this was more educational than the duties he was laden with. He immediately signed up for the course without even bothering to get the okay from anyone.

That night he waited until after supper to spring the good news. His parents eyed each other before focusing back to him. The silence alone was nerve-racking. Wasn't anyone going to speak, offer a suggestion, and yell...well?

His daddy got up from his chair and paced the floor twice before sitting back down. He rubbed a hand over his chin. "Mike, are you sure this is what you really want?"

"Yes, sir," he answered, like an obedient young soldier.

"You realize you may have to stay after school on occasion and help out with the projects?"

Excitement bubbled inside of him. *Yes, yes, yes,* this was the moment he was waiting for, when his dad would say, no more chores, or no more having to do all his homework. A huge light went off in his brain as he beamed from ear to ear.

"Yes sir, Daddy, you bet."

"All right then, it's settled, if that is what you truly want."

Mike nodded his head rapidly.

"You must remember that your chores will be waiting when you arrive home, along with any homework. Or anything else your mother and I may need you to help us with."

Funny how a little anticipation of excitement can quickly, dissipate from a young boy's body. Had they forgotten that he wasn't the only child in the family? Evidently so.

This time Mike fell silent as he stared at the papers on the table. What could he say? He had already signed up for the class. If he backed out now, surely his parents would think something amiss. Under his breath he sighed, a painful moan, allowing no one to hear but himself. He had been defeated— again. When was he, the child, ever going to win a case?

"Yes, Daddy, I bear that in mind, more than you know."

The words poured painfully from his lips, as if being forced. With head lowered and hands folded behind his back, he walked off to his room and climbed under the covers. No sense in crying over spilled milk. What was done was done.

The days that followed weren't too bad. Luckily he wasn't flooded with homework or chores. The afternoons he had the meetings were the best. He learned so many new things in life.

The most memorable moment came when he first set his eyes on Bridget. She was an absolute doll. The class had taken a trip to the county fair where the farmed animals were housed, and one look at her prompted a thumping of love in his heart. She was by far the most beautiful little pig he had ever seen. It was love at first sight. She was all black with white shoulders.

Each child who chose to have one of the little piggies could take one home. Naturally, Mike was the first to raise his hand. He wanted Bridget and no one had better get in his way.

When the man handed her to Mike, she squealed, as Mike hugged her in delight. This was something that was actually his and no one else's. He had never owned anything where he was the sole possessor. As he walked out of the auditorium he felt on top of the world. For a moment, he wondered if this was how a mother felt when she was first able to cuddle her newborn infant.

When he arrived home, he realized that he'd failed to consider what his daddy's reaction would be once he entered with the tiny pig. Fortunately, the director had gotten to him first and explained the situation. In the backyard, his daddy had installed a small fence for one said pig.

Mike really hugged his dad that day for the first time. Never had he known the man to care enough to do such a nice deed for him. After all the many whippings and previous incidents with him, Mike was sure he frowned upon him being his son. He soon discovered he was completely off track. The only thing he enforced was, since she was his pet, she was thus his responsibility.

He quickly found out owning a pet could not only be fun, but also time consuming, not to mention costly. It was always bathe her, feed her, and clean up after her. He would look at his mother and wonder, did she ever feel in the same boat with her children? He hugged Bridget and told her he loved her. His thoughts had reminded him what he was doing for her was done out of love, like a parent with a child.

The big day came to enter her in the FFA contest, for the prize for best pig in the valley. Bridget had to be the winner by far, he was constantly boasting.

He gave her a bath the night before and brushed her little hair down. Mother had some baby powder so he shook a little on her skin to make her smell good. He stood admiring her beauty. This young boy was so proud of his pet. No sooner had he turned his back than Bridget took a turn for the corner, and ran out of the house, straight into the backyard. By the time he got outside, she was wallowing in the wet dirt and ruining her nice refreshing scent. How could she do this to him? All his efforts had been in vain. She enjoyed the filth more than being clean.

The morning of the contest was radiantly beautiful. The sun was shining brightly, not a dark cloud in sight. Quickly, Mike scurried out of bed, threw on his clothes, then ran out to get Bridget, who was curled up like a comfortable fat cat lounging after a huge meal. He gave her another bath and rubbed her down in powder before brushing her thin strands of hair. The white streaks around her shoulders stood out, illuminating her beauty. He placed a tiny pink ribbon around her neck. His mother had given it to him special to put on her for this special day.

Billy and Mike climbed in the back of the 1948 Ford pickup, while they patiently waited for their parents and the others to hurry and climb in for the ride. Mike was on pins and needles wanting to get to the fair on time. Bridget had to be the first to be entered in the contest.

The ride had been shorter than the waiting at the fair

grounds. Bridget was placed in a small cage, so she wouldn't get in the dirt. After she won, he would allow her to roam in all the dirt her little heart desired. The time finally arrived for the judging. His heart pumped furiously as he waited as patiently as he knew how for the winner to be announced. Bridget didn't win first place, but she did come in second. The judge handed him a pretty blue ribbon and said she was indeed a beautiful pig.

That was the last day he ever saw his pet pig. A farmer asked if he might purchase her and take her to live on his huge farm. She would feel more at home with his other pigs. At first Mike couldn't bear the thought of giving her up. He had cared for her practically from birth, but he knew, being the only little pig, she probably could stand some company. He hugged her one last time before handing her to the farmer.

In the quiet of his room that night, he held the blue ribbon in his hand and recalled his fondest memories of Bridget. She was nothing like a dog or cat, but she had indeed been his pet. One that he had been most proud to own and raise for what time he had her in his possession. It had also been a time that had brought his father closer to him. Moments of a *journey* that he would never forget during his lifetime.

Give Me That Old Time Religion
The Payback

Mike could never understand why he insisted on tagging along with Bryan, even after Bryan beat up on him the way that he did. He was two years older than Mike, not the oldest of the children, but the second in line, and for some reason, Mike felt compelled to drag along with him wherever he went or follow directly in his steps.

As he reflected upon it all later, he realized it must have really been love that he felt for the brother. For some strange reason, Bryan could get away with whatever obstacle crossed his path, even when it came to receiving a trip to the woodshed.

Their daddy had a can of Carnation Milk he always used to sweeten his coffee. Bryan insisted that Mike drink some of it, telling him how good it was, and like any naive child he fell for Bryan's scam. Of course, daddy wasn't too happy the next morning when he discovered half of the can empty. It was something he couldn't always afford to buy. And when he did, he used it sparingly. Mike made the bad mistake of listening to his brother Bryan and drank some of the milk. That was his first mistake. The second was telling on Bryan.

The spanking Bryan received was nothing compared to

the intense dark look he cast over Mike, after returning from the woodshed. Daddy had tanned Bryan's bottom good for coaxing him into drinking that milk. And Mike knew that Bryan always managed to get out of going to that woodshed. Unfortunately, this time, he was unlucky.

What he didn't realize was that Bryan was going to make him pay for that little error, and make Mike realize if he ever tattled on him anymore, he would have to suffer the consequences. Bryan waited for his chance. He waited until their parents were out of the house, then he entered the living room, sporting daddy's belt. The belt buckle was in itself a torture if one was ever struck with it.

Bryan stood in the center of the room, pulling and cracking the ends together, smiling wickedly as the ends popped loudly. His face reminded Mike of those fire-breathing dragons he so often read about in myths.

"Just had to spill the beans didn't you, Mike?" he inquired smartly as if in charge.

Mike's frail body started to tremble, but he didn't allow him to notice. "You better put daddy's belt away, before you ruin it. He will take you back to the woodshed."

"And who is going to tell on me this time? You, perhaps?" He paced around the room, still popping the belt in mid-air. "I'm going to teach you a lesson, Mike, my boy. One that you will remember for the rest of your life. Next time you won't be so quick to tattle to daddy about his milk."

He swung the belt once, striking Mike's right leg. Mike quickly jumped from the couch and ran toward the front door as another fly of the belt sent the edge of the buckle straight into his back. His scream echoed loudly through the house as he reached for the doorknob.

The door opened and their daddy entered just as Bryan was about to hit Mike's back. One stare from daddy's glaring black eyes sent Bryan into shock. Never had he expected his dad's early return.

The scared look on Mike's face expressed it all. Bryan knew he wouldn't be telling on him this time. Daddy had witnessed the end of the trauma. One yank of the belt from Bryan's hand, and Daddy was pulling him by the ear out to the woodshed. Daddy was ranting as Bryan struggled with him. Mike could hear him shouting all the way inside.

"Let me get something across to you right now, *son*. If anyone is doing any spankings in this household it will either be your mother or me. You are never to take matters into your hands like this again. Am I making myself clear, Bryan?"

"Yes," he whined in pain.

The remainder of the month nothing was said concerning the episode with Bryan, but Mike had a gut feeling that Bryan would surprise him with something gloomy when he wasn't looking over his shoulder.

That cold, darkened night arrived as Bryan invited him to go to a church gathering. He was taken by surprise. Bryan, who hated the word religion, was requesting his presence at a church social. What was this world coming to? Never did he expect anything to happen at a church building, so Mike changed his clothes and joined him outside.

The night air was brisk and breezy as they walked along the pathway. They carried on a casual conversation like two old friends who had been apart for a long time. It was almost as if the old Bryan was back. Mike had missed those times together.

The building was rather big, painted white, with a huge

bell that hung on the edge of the side. As they entered the doors, they saw that the room was full of people. He couldn't really count all of them, but there had to be over a hundred for sure. Bryan took Mike's hand and they went toward the middle of the room finding a couple of empty seats. The others would turn and smile, or cast them a frown, almost as if to question if they were lost.

The pews were filling up fast. There was an old rundown piano that sat in the corner of the room in front of them. The podium, as Bryan called it, was a few inches off the floor. Before he knew what was happening, a heavyset man sporting a fuzzy beard hopped on top of the stage and began saying words, sort of like a sermon.

His speech grew louder as others in the audience agreed with an "Amen, brother, tell it like it is." Even the women were blabbering in the background. All of a sudden, hands were waving, everyone was shouting and speaking gibberish like this boy had never heard in his life. Mike didn't know about Bryan, but he was scared. He wanted to get out of there. When he looked in Bryan's direction, he sat eyeing the crowd, taking in all their actions.

"Bryan, let's go home. I don't want to be here any longer."

Mike tugged at his arm, but Bryan couldn't hear him for the confusion of shouting noise. His bladder began to send off an alarm in his system as he felt the urge...no, the need to get to a bathroom, in a hurry. He reached over and took a hold of Bryan's ear.

"Bryan, I've got to pee!" He practically screamed the words in his ears.

Bryan waited a minute before he answered. He scanned

the area, as if to look for the facilities, then he nodded for Mike to go toward the front. Mike looked in that direction and he froze. That was where some of the others were standing in a circle with raised hands, swaying back and forth as if in some trance. He continued nodding his head in that area. He was more scared to move than to wet his pants. There was no way he wanted to get near that circle of women. He sat for a moment, considering his outcome. If he allowed the urine to flow through his breeches, that would be an embarrassing situation for this eight-year-old boy, but if he ventured toward the circle, one of those old ladies might grab him, pulling him in.

His bladder chose for him. Quickly he jumped from the seat and ran toward the front. What he had anticipated, happened.

There was no bathroom in the front of the church building. The whole thing had been a set up. The women took hold of him and pulled him closer. They kept chanting they had to save him from Satan. Some brother Bryan had turned out to be. This was his way of getting back at him for that little tattling with the milk, and he had taken full advantage of the situation.

Mike began crying so loud that one of the women pulled him out and tried to console him, but he refused to listen. Instead, he broke free from her clutches and ran out of the building as fast as his feet would carry him. He didn't bother looking for Bryan. He didn't care to know where he was. This little episode had been the last straw for this young boy.

As Mike approached the front yard, he noticed Bryan perched on the front steps of the porch. He was smiling from ear to ear. Mike never said one word to him about that night.

Bryan could tell by Mike's expression that he was extremely upset and angry. Mike cast him one hateful look of contempt before he raced to the bathroom. All the events that had transpired had allowed his mind to forget his kidneys. He found it a wonder that his breeches weren't dampened and soiled after such a commotion, but luckily for him, everything had stayed intact. He was almost positive that Bryan had wished he had messed his breeches, so daddy would have taken him to the woodshed.

That was Mike's last encounter with that type of religion. He sort of stayed away from any church going, unless his mother forced it upon him. His parents were never told of that one night. He figured that Bryan finally felt pacified since he no longer sought to get back at him for anything.

After the Laughter, Comes the Rain
The Separation...Saying Goodbye

Every time he observed a rainbow after a heavy shower, he would always try to look toward the end for that pot of gold that his granddad would so often insist lies on the other side. It didn't matter how hard he tried to look, he never saw it. The only pot of gold of happiness he ever witnessed was within the circle of their family. The times always seemed tough, with money scarce and jobs short, but his parents provided for the necessary things he and his siblings needed in life.

It wasn't until after the episode with Marvetta that his mother began to feel ill. At the time, he had no reason to expect any doom arising in their midst. That fear of separation or something happening to any one in his family was never considered.

Bryan, David and Mike were in the back throwing the ball when they heard Marvetta scream. She was only two and a half years old at the time and insisted in playing in any dirt that her bottom chose to land in. The scream frightened them. They turned to see of her whereabouts. She was sitting by the torn fence, not too far away, shaking her small body, as if to remove anything that was covering her skin.

David was the first to get to her. The tiny tot was covered in red stinging ants doing a Mexican hat dance on her flesh. Mother ran out of the house to see what the commotion was all about. When she saw Marvetta covered with the tiny creatures, she took her from David, and quickly removed the clothes from her body, while trying to knock any of the insects off.

"Bryan, run get me some cold water, a rag and alcohol."

He stood frozen, unable to move because of the predicament of his little sister. Mother took one look at him and only had to repeat herself once. "BRYAN, NOW!" her voice commanded.

He raced toward the house. Within seconds he was back with everything that mother had requested.

She hurried and washed off Marvetta's red little body, before applying some of the alcohol. Sister began screaming worse with the application of the cold liquid. Mother would try to console her, but the tiny tot continued to weep alligator tears.

She took her inside and ripped an old sheet in half to wrap around her body. She instructed Bryan to watch the house and the other children, as she held tightly to Marvetta. Her cries echoed for the whole neighborhood to hear.

"Mike, you and David come with me," Mother said with a trembling voice.

Doctor Sturki was a kind old gent who got along with just about anybody. If anyone had an ailment, the man had a cure. He was short, round and bald, with a few strands of hair that lay on top of his head. Except for the doctor who had performed surgery on Mike's ears, Dr. Sturki had been the only other doctor he remembered ever going to.

David and Mike waited outside on the steps of the doctor's office while Mother took Marvetta inside. The front window to his office was open, so they were able to hear a little of what was going on. For a while her crying could still be heard from the waiting room, but after the nurse saw the problem, she quickly told Mother to carry her into the back.

They wondered what could be taking so long. It seemed like they had waited for hours and hours. The sound of Marvetta's crying had long vanished when she went into the back office.

Mike got up from the steps and made a start for the door when mother walked out. Marvetta's tiny arms were clasped around her neck, as if she were holding on for life. Her face was red from all the tears.

"Come on boys; let's take your sister home."

Mike eyed his mother curiously. Was there something she wasn't informing them? "Mom, will...will she be all right?"

"Yes, Mike. He rubbed a lotion on her and gave her a mild shot. I have some medicine to give her when we get home."

Something was not right with Mother. She looked pale and appeared withdrawn. It was more than the accident of ants with Marvetta. Her features were not what they ought to be. A couple of months later the symptoms began to show.

One evening when Daddy got home after a hard day and went over to hug Mother, he commented how feverish she felt. She remarked it was probably the flu going around and continued cooking supper. When everyone sat down at the table, Mother didn't eat. Instead, she said her body needed to rest for a spell. All Mike saw was what was stamped all over his dad's face: concern. Of course, he wasn't the only one that was troubled over their mother. They had never seen her this tired. With all of the children, she was active and on the go, from the time she arose until the time her head hit the pillow at night.

As the weeks continued to shift and change course for everyone around, so did Mother. She grew paler, ate less, lost weight, and either was running a fever or enduring hot sweats at night. Mike was certain that his tenth birthday would brighten the day, seeing her son turn another year older and learning more about life. He had been mistaken. It was apparent her illness was growing worse. Doctor Sturki had prescribed antibiotics and other medicies, but nothing was bringing Mother back to herself.

When Marvetta turned three, Mother baked her a cake. She decorated it beautifully for her only daughter. She wanted everything to be perfect. After finally getting Marvetta to blow out the candles, Mother was overcome with a spell of dizziness. Then she fainted, falling to the floor. Daddy rushed to her side.

Robert wet a cold cloth and placed it on Mother's forehead. Still nothing. There was a pulse, Daddy informed them, but it was racing. Hurriedly he picked her up and carried her to the pickup. Since Robert was the oldest of the boys, he instructed him to drive to the hospital, while he clung tightly to their Mother.

When the old '48 Ford pulled out of sight, they eyed each another as a pain-stricken sigh of fear overcame them. Marvetta was too young to realize what was taking place. She continued to work with her cake, making a mess, giggling little giggles as she playfully hit the fork against the edge of the saucer.

Bryan, David and Mike sat on the couch, not saying a word, while Benjamin and William ate some more of Marvetta's cake. Mike wondered if Benjamin, who was now eight, and William, five, really understood what had taken place. To them, Mother had only taken ill and needed to go to the doctor. Of course, Mike, who had just turned ten, thought his dear Mother just had the flu, too. It was what Daddy had said. It had to be.

The wait they had to endure was a lot longer than the afternoon all the ants covered Marvetta's body. They were growing impatient waiting for Robert or even Daddy to come home and tell them anything of Mother's ailment. He remembered David putting Marvetta and the two smaller boys to bed, then rejoining Bryan and him on the couch. They all looked like they needed to be in bed themselves, but the thoughts of their precious mother weighed heavily on their hearts and minds.

By early morning, their eyes gave way to sleep. When their daddy walked in, they were still lying on the couch clinging to each other. Bryan was the first to open his eyes. He shook them, waking them from their slumber. One quick look at Daddy told them he hadn't been able to get a wink of sleep during the night. Beneath his tired eyes were swollen bags. He sat down in his huge arm chair.

Daddy raked a hand through his hair. "Are the other children in bed?"

"Yes, Daddy," David answered. "Did Robert stay with Mother?"

"I asked him to until I can rearrange my hours with the boss. The doctor said it would be all right."

"Daddy, is Mother...is she...?" But the words would not come out of David's mouth. Tears began misting his eyes.

"She is in the hospital...for now. The doctor is uncertain as to the exact diagnosis, but there is one factor he is concentrating on. He won't know for sure until after all the tests are finished and even then..."

Daddy broke into tears, unable to finish his sentence. Bryan, David and Mike looked at each other, not knowing how to react. Never had they seen the backbone of their family, the man who carried all the strength, break down and weep in front of them. They were silent for a long time.

By the end of the week the doctor was absolutely positive of Mother's illness: tuberculosis. The word alone meant doom to the family. Daddy was not himself anymore. The older brothers, along with Mike, had to care for the younger children as well as themselves. All they could think about was the fate and possible crisis awaiting their family.

They were allowed to see Mother one time while she was hospitalized. There was a very kind nurse who allowed them entry to Mother's room when no one was around. The visit had to be short due to her frail condition. Her appearance alone was a shock. She had become thinner, and there was hardly any color in her face. It was extremely hard to accept this woman as their mother.

Mike remembered she spoke to them one at a time that day. He had always felt a close bond to his mother. He didn't know if it was because he was the middle child or because he felt she had always been there for all his obstacles. The closeness was just there. He feared her slipping away as she spoke to him. The words were very soft, an audible whisper almost, but he made sure to take heed to every word she uttered.

A mere boy of ten needed both a mother and a father. Not only him, but the other ones as well. What would they do without a mother? He prayed with all the energy he had in his heart that she would improve, get better and come home to live with them for the rest of their lives.

By the end of the month there was nothing else to do, no doctors, no hope, and no prayers, rather sorrow. Their dear mother had died. She was being taken away from all of them. Mike's heart shattered into so many pieces he was unable to think or focus on any of his brothers, and…Marvetta. Oh, no, he had forgotten about their little sister. She had only been with mother for three short years. The only baby daughter mother had given birth to would be without a mother.

He wondered what would become of them. There was no way that their daddy could handle or care for them and work. Knowing him, he wouldn't leave them to care for themselves while he was away at work. It was bad enough that he had to leave them to care for each other while their mother had been in the hospital. Mike's mind seemed to be playing a double turn. His mother had not even been lowered into the ground and all he could dwell on was the outcome of the seven of them.

Running to his bed, he stretched across the covers and cried until there were no more tears left. He recalled the others shed tears as well. Marvetta would cry for her mother. She didn't understand the whole mess. All she knew was the lovely, warm woman who use to rock her to sleep at night, or hold her warmly during the day while she baked cookies, or cater to her whenever her little eyes would look up at her, was no longer there.

"Mama, mama," were her constant words. But there

would be no more *mama* for any of them. Mike's only worry now was, just where they would end up going.

Daddy left it up to them to view the casket. He had heard some people comment children should never view a dead body, especially of a loved one, but he didn't pay them any mind. He spoke to them, as if adults. They all agreed they wanted to see their beloved mother one more time.

Daddy remarked he wouldn't feel right if he didn't at least take Marvetta to see her mother one last time. She clung tightly to his neck as they both viewed Mother's resting body. Tears streamed from his eyes as he eyed his little girl.

It was the hardest day of his life holding his little daughter in his arms as they said goodbye to the one beautiful woman they both loved. "Honey, we have to tell Mama goodbye. She's gone to another place to live. She had to go away for now, but you still have Daddy. I will be here for you, sweetheart," he spoke through tears.

Marvetta's little green eyes gazed down at her mother as she waved her little hand in a goodbye motion. She didn't understand a word Daddy had said. All she observed was her mother sleeping peacefully, just like she was all the mornings she would walk into her bedroom at the crack of dawn and wake her up. It never dawned on her that she would never see her in this life anymore.

The day of the burial, rain was in the forecast. It was only a drizzle as they stood out in the cemetery. Daddy only wanted a graveside service. He didn't think he could hold up to a long funeral service in a church building. Seeing his children, without their mother, was more than enough for him to have to endure. This was what his loving wife would have wanted.

Mike remembered seeing relatives he never knew they had. It reminded him of termites coming out of woodwork, there were so many. They would walk up to all of them, showering them with hugs, condolences and their deepest respect for their loss. All Mike thought of was his mother lying in that cold, dark box—alone—with no one. Soon she would be lowered into the ground. Never would he be held in her arms again, or run to her when he had a problem. He was only ten. He needed her. Didn't anyone understand that? Didn't anyone understand they all needed her?

He had no use for any of these relatives. He wanted his mother. In his mind, he screamed as loud as his insides would allow—*MOTHER, WHY?* The tears came again. He didn't care who saw him. All he wanted was the warm, loving woman back who had given him birth!

New Beginning
Recalling Old Memories

The warm rays of July's sun reflected on the window of the car as he got out and strolled over to the graves. It had been a good ten years since he had last visited this site. He bent and looked at his mother's grave, which only now carried a headstone. All the children had pitched in to place one on her grave. There had not been enough money to furnish one at the time of her death.

His mind went back to the last time he stood in this exact spot. Only a young boy of ten with a family he knew and loved more than life. After Mother's death, all the children had been split up and sent to other homes. The connection of the family had been broken. His father's constant companion and friend had been a bottle and any woman who would allow him to lay his head on their pillow at night.

The promise he had made to sweet Marvetta of always being there had been severed not long after their mother had been placed in the cold, dark earth. Mike knew the heartbreak had been hard on all of them, but couldn't their dad have been strong enough with all his children to keep the family ties together?

A few of the other brothers had stayed in touch with him,

especially Bryan. As for Marvetta, two of the brothers had spoken to her by phone occasionally, but Mike had not seen her anymore after the burial and the dividing of the siblings. Only two of the brothers, Bryan and William, had seen more of the little sister. As he continued bending, gazing at the head stone, he was unaware that even in his future years, he would not ever see his dear sister. In his search, he would try to locate her, but his efforts would be unfruitful.

He would have to accept the fact that the only time he was able to see his baby sister was during the short three years they shared in their home. That was the only time he was able to spend with the loving angel. So many times he had wondered how she was doing with the family that adopted her, but that was something that he would never find out in his lifetime. Marvetta was gone, and none of the brothers later in life would be able to trace her steps.

In his mind he retraced the steps that led to the disorder of his life and his brethren. Who knew that after being born into this world one would have to endure such agonizing pain? It was a journey that wasn't even over, yet had inflicted much pain on him. He was sure there would be more in his life span.

His mother's sister already supported five children of her own, but she had agreed to care for him and Bryan if it came down to them needing a place to stay. David and Robert were tossed from home to home, while Benjamin and William continued to be passed around, causing trouble, then transported off and on into a juvenile facility. Marvetta was the only one who had stayed with a permanent, grounded family. In his distance from all of them, he had remained in contact with a minimum of letters, only through a couple of his brothers and his aunt. He had been told Marvetta only tolerated the people with whom she had been sheltered and as soon as she became of age, she would be high tailing it for parts unknown. He had never been able to hear the real story from his sweet sister's lips.

He had often wondered if Daddy had been more understanding to all of them after Mother's death whether they would have maintained that once close knit family Even to this day, he hated what his father had enforced upon each of them.

As he looked back now, he was almost positive it was his mother who was the backbone and strength of the family. He didn't believe the words *coping* and *caring* for your children were even in his father's vocabulary. With her deceased, his father's parental duties seemed to be shoveled with dirt in the ground alongside her.

Wiping the few tears that had begun to fall from his eyes, he rose to his feet. There was one more grave he had to visit before his departure.

The headstone carried the words, *Beloved David*. He was the first of the children, three years older than Mike. He had died in a terrible automobile accident one night returning from work. The date Mike would never forget, April first, known by so many as April Fool's Day. He had enlisted in the Army and was away in training when his aunt notified him of the tragedy. At first he considered it a joke, but as he pondered on the matter, he knew she wouldn't be joking about something so tragic.

He ran his finger over the carved engraving as he eyed yet another Fairmont grave. His survivors had been a wife, a son and a daughter. He wondered how many more family members would soon be entering the darkness of the cold earth.

He recalled the time David was given a new pair of black loafers. After running around half the time barefoot, he had been so proud of the new shoes. He would polish them, brush them off so not to collect dust or dirt and place them lovingly beside his bed. Mike failed to watch his steps and tripped clumsily, bending the top of them. David instantly retrieved them from the floor. The loafers' were still glossy, but his brother's little accident had bent the toe, making a crease in the shoe.

David became very irate over that little mishap, scolding him for ruining his shoes. Mike tried explaining they were still new, not ruined at all, but David saw it differently.

The brother continued eyeing the grave as love entered in his heart. Releasing a heavy sigh, he clung to that memory as he thought so lovingly of his older brother. More than anything, he wished he could have seen him one last time before his untimely death.

The tears had subsided by the time he got near the car. There was one last look cast toward the graves before he left to visit a while with his aunt. She had been like a second mother to him during his troubled mourning. Often he had wanted to call her mother, instead of Auntie Irene, but his inner conscious never permitted it.

Uncle Harold had by far been more of a daddy to him than his own had. At least he had never shut him out. He always spared time for him, as if he were one of his own flesh-and-blood sons. He was sure if Aunt and Uncle hadn't allowed him or Bryan to stay with them, no doubt, they would have been termed *troublemakers* and allowed to spend some time behind bars.

The slow drive by the old homestead brought to his mind

memories of yesteryear. Another couple occupied the home the family once shared. The house had even been repainted and renovated. He parked the car, leaving it to idle for a few moments, while he visualized the scene in his head. Mother would be hanging the clothes on the line while the boys played tag or threw the ball at one another.

There was a glimpse of Daddy coming in from a long day at the coal mine going up to mother, caressing her soft body, and giving her a kiss on the lips.

"What are you boys looking at?" he would always inquire with a laugh.

The house had never been huge, but seeing it today, after all these years, made it appear incredibly smaller. It had been their second home, after Daddy had received a bonus and raise in his check. The first house, he recalled, had only a dirt floor. They had been ecstatic to finally leave that small shell of a dwelling. At least in their second home they had their own bed and all the floors had been wood.

There was a loud scream from a small boy that brought him back to reality. Turning his head, he glanced at two boys chasing one another, playing dodge ball. He was beginning to feel a lump start to mount in his throat. It was time to go, leave this place. Why had he bothered coming back? All it did was dredge up painful memories that could never be corrected.

Driving through the town of Logan, he realized that a lot had changed since his days as a small child, not only with his old home, but with the neighborhood as well. A new school had been constructed, expanded shopping centers, a playground, a few more hotels and inns. Yes, the town was rapidly growing with the times. Funny how the time had speedily flown by.

Looking at his watch, he realized it was getting late. He would only have a couple of hours to spend reminiscing with his aunt and uncle before he would have to leave for South Carolina. With his basic training behind him, the Army was now sending him to Germany for a year. Time to stop gazing at the scenery. Moving the gear into drive and putting a little more pressure on the gas pedal, he climbed to the speed limit—destination, home at last with Aunt and Uncle.

Closing the door to memories of the past, he focused his thoughts on the present. The past was only a mere shadow as the car edged completely away from the house that he once called home.

Brenda Lou, How Are You?
Dear John?

Mike lost his virginity when he turned fifteen. The high school boys would all kid one another, insisting that if you never had a girl you weren't much of a boy. Looking back now, he knew all of the talk was pressure to be with the in crowd. If you didn't smoke cigarettes, or talk big, or sleep with a girl every weekend, face it, you were considered unpopular. The kids of today were no different from his era. If there was something new to do, most of them would jump at the chance to try it.

He developed a taste for cigarettes when he was twelve and had smoked ever since. As for girls, after that first time at the school dance, he would go out with them occasionally, but he never forced himself on girls, or constantly harassed them, like the other boys did just to demonstrate their masculinity.

Gladys Simers wasn't what you would classify as beautiful, but if boys needed a first time, she willingly offered her services. While the other girls bragged about their slim, trim figures and shapely bust lines, she, on the other hand, was rather short, plump, and not too attractive, but her beauty far exceeded her outward features. Hers was from within.

Some of Mike's friends insisted he go over and ask her

out to the dance, but Mike would shy away from women. For a long time he had distanced himself from the opposite sex, not wanting to commit to anyone or anything for fear of loss. Every time he got attached to someone they would leave him, never to return. Not long after his mother's death, his father, not able to care for the children, sought the children homes at a nearby orphanage. There were a few family members who were able to care for the offspring, but some still ended up in orphanages.

When Mike was unable to stay with his aunt much, that had turned him against getting close to any women. It left a sour trail for him to follow. The people were not nice in those homes. Sure they appeared nice on the outside but once you were left alone and the family member gone, it was like a prison. After he'd gotten into a lot of trouble, the institution could no longer deal with Mike. Aunt and Uncle would have to take the young man into his home. Either that or confine him to a cell in the closest jail. He was glad when they took him from that terrible dungeon. His father had taken a complete turnaround with all the children. He was afraid the rest of his life was doomed forever. Then his teen years happened to take a turn. That was when his friends insisted he see Gladys.

Gladys was ready for any young boy who wanted to release any tension that he might be feeling. After constant badgering and harassment from his friends, he gave in and spoke to Gladys. Instantly, she agreed to accompany him to the dance. No one else had bothered to ask and probably no one would, he silently thought.

After one slow dance, he asked if she would take a stroll with him. Eagerly her eyes and lips said yes. They walked past the school to a nearby old run down store and hid behind the building. He felt shy, awkward, and excessively clumsy. Gladys sensed he was nervous and understood, slowly taking matters into her hands.

Her hands glided freely over his body, as warmness surged through parts of him, leaving a slight tingle he'd never experienced before. Her lips searched for his mouth, and upon reaching the young tender virgin lips, she kissed him as her tongue slivered like a snake in his mouth. The sensation was enough to rupture his brain. He thought of checking his eyes to make sure they hadn't popped from their sockets.

When they fell to the ground, and she roamed his flesh, he squealed with delight. She permitted him to caress her at times, but since it was his first time ever with a female, she took complete charge of his body, making sure he received every possible sensation she could stimulate, causing an electric flow of current to send him shooting off fireworks never before fired or lit in his lifetime. When the last missile ignited and shot into space, he pulled her tight against his chest, as he shivered with a trembling sensation never felt before. Oh, yes, this was by far greater than any ride on a roller coaster. This rush was a record all time high.

Afterwards, she boosted his morale tremendously by remarking how fabulous he had been. That night had indeed left a mark on the young man, one he remembered, always.

As the days pushed on, there had been a few other girls in his life as he grew older, but only one stood out. Brenda Lou Felding, medium height, short curly brown hair, a few tiny specks of freckles distributed on her face, and lovely green eyes. They felt a mutual attraction for each other. This girl was far different from any other he had dated.

He loved her...a lot. They had even discussed marriage, but it was during a time he was, yet again, being transferred overseas and she wanted to wait for his return.

Her parents were equally fond of Mike. They were so fond of him that they went as far as allowing him to stay over, in her bed, to spend the night. They were sort of an open type of family. He was the second boy she had ever been with, but the only one she truly shared deep feelings for. When he left for Vietnam, she was heartbroken, but the letters they wrote to one another kept their hearts tied to each other until his return.

The year seemed to fly by. The duty was different from any other job he had ever encountered, but Brenda's incoming letters helped him with his struggle in the foreign land. A few months before his estimated time of departure, the letters slowed down.

Brenda had always insisted on writing all the time to him, but for some reason, her letters had slowed to a crawl in his mail system. A lot of the guys claimed it was due to his time being so short, while others insisted she had found another *John* to spend her hours with. Mike believed the first over the later. He loved Brenda and her feelings for him were mutual. She would never dump him for another guy.

His first visit back in the states was naturally paid upon his grandmother, who had kept in touch with him off and on. The second was with Brenda. He had been told she indeed had found another young man to bide her time with. Mike said he had to hear it from her lips before he actually believed it.

When her arms wrapped around his body and their lips met after being apart for the year, he noticed a difference; something was lacking on her part. They sat on the porch swing and she expounded all the details to him, as best as she could. She didn't wish to hurt his feelings, but she had fallen in love with another.

There was a good deal of hurt felt but he would not permit her to even catch a glimpse of it. Rather, he behaved as if he were pleased for her that she had found her one true love to spend the rest of her life with. At least they would not jump into a marriage that would face gloom down the road. The worst blow arrived when he inquired about the lucky fellow. He would like to shake his hand, *more like break his neck,* he thought, but he wouldn't admit that to her. When she uttered his name, it took all the self-restraint he had to keep from choking her and getting a gun to blow his head off.

"Paul Wagnall." She spoke softly, as if afraid to speak.

Good ole Paul, his closest and very best friend. No sooner then his back is turned, Paul is dating his girl, and undoubtedly bumping heavily with her when he is away, probably in her own bed, too, with her parent's consent.

The blood in his body wanted to boil, as he sensed his pressure already rising high enough to pop a cork on a powder keg. But he refrained from any harsh actions. *Take it like a good soldier,* he reasoned. *Chalk up another vanished female, Mike.* He should have known better to give his heart to another, but like an idiot, he had fallen prey to true love. Well, no more! All that stuff was for the birds. He had no time to be flying, searching for another female to drop him like a worm!

He was finished, thoroughly finished with women! Use 'em and leave 'em would be his motto. Maybe the other boys he had attended school with were right when they chose to continuously mess around with anything that wore a skirt. He would give it a try.

Any sensation he felt now was lingering hurt. One that he feared would ever go away. In time he would seek out and find the one real woman who would love him for what he was, who would seek to put his feelings and desires before hers.

Yes, there would be a woman as loving and understanding as his own mother one day for him, but at the present, he knew not what the future held, and he didn't wish to go looking for any female companionship.

The only things his pale green eyes were seeing clearly were the heartaches and pain.

Young Man Where Was Your Head?
The Rooster

Okay, so maybe trying to smuggle a rooster into the BOQ wasn't the smartest move of a young private's career, but there were extenuating circumstances. Mike kept replaying that message over and over in his head but it wasn't registering. It had been a stupid move on his part to try to get back at his drill sergeant in those terms. But face it. He was a new recruit. He knew the man didn't like him.

Here he was a teenage boy, just entering the military, in a new location far away from his aunt and uncle. He wondered why he had even enlisted. Why? Because he had been stupid to listen to the recruiting officer when he explained all the benefits that he would be receiving. This wasn't like going to the FFA when he was a small boy and trying to get out of chores. This was something really serious. So why had he even gone to that recruiting office?

"Big bucks. Extended vacations. A new life you've never experienced. Education benefits. Believe me, you can't pass up this opportunity," the recruiting officer had said, elaborating with a huge grin.

Yeah that was something that Mike had remembered. That man grinning from ear to ear as he handed him the pa-

pers. As he thought on it now, the man wasn't too profes-
sional. More like a grown man who still had a lot of growing
up to do. But the more he listened to him, the more he
seemed to twirl in his spider's web. So he signed up. He supposed in the back of his mind, he figured they would find a
flaw and not accept him. Boy had he been wrong.

In no time, he was in the Army and headed straight for
Ft. Benning, Georgia. Of course he wasn't the only one.
There were a lot of new trainees that he would be bunking
with. Oh boy, oh joy, he thought.

When he got off the bus, he inhaled deeply. Maybe all
this would end up being smooth sailing. Like a picnic. The six
weeks would fly by. Then he could say goodbye to this southern fort and head back to the great state of Ohio.

Unfortunately his training wasn't the picnic he thought it
would be. It was swarming in red fire ants. The drill sergeant
was a monster. Mike was sure that Attila the Hun was Tweety
Bird compared to this man.

The man was only five-feet-eight inches with about one
hundred sixty-five pounds to his frame. Not much bigger than
Mike himself, but when the man spoke, it was like a great
whirlwind. That short-statured man carried a punch. No one
had better get in his way; that was for certain. Where was this
drill sergeant the day he signed up for the Army? One word
from his mouth and Mike would have been out of that recruiting office like a streak of lightning.

"I'm your new drill sergeant. You'll call me Sgt. Lambert. For the next six weeks, you and I will be like ham on
rye. What I say goes. I'm here to turn you little boys into
grown men. Now get your stuff into your barracks and unload
those duffel bags!"

Okay. Where were Aunt and Uncle when he could really use them? Where was that bus that had dropped everyone off? He wished he could get a hold of that recruiting officer. He truly believed at that point, he would have given that man a new face-lift.

Needless to say his training was something that Mike never expected. He went to bed sore. When it was time to get out of the bunk, he was like a stiff board. Day in and day out his life was miserable. It seemed like the drill sergeant was making his stay unbearable. He had to think of a way to get out of this crazy hole.

"Fairmont!" Sgt. Lambert bellowed.

"Yes sir," he quickly answered as he came to attention.

"What are you gawking at?"

"Nothing, sir. I needed to take a breather."

"Do you see the other men stopping from their run?"

"No, sir."

"Then get the lead out of your butt and get those legs moving!"

Mike eyed him.

"Now, Fairmont! Not tomorrow, but now!"

"Yes, Sergeant," he said as his legs took off like hot molten lava flowing. With every step he took, he thought of Drill Sgt. Lambert. He pictured him as a tiny ant under each step he took. He was determined to crush him over and over.

It was on a sunny afternoon that Mike overheard two other privates discussing the drill sergeant. As he polished away at his Army boots, he made sure that his ear stretched enough to overhear their conversation.

"I can't wait to leave this outfit," Smith said.

"You got that right," Williams agreed.

"I heard a couple of other trainees saying they needed a way to get Sgt. Lambert off their backs, too. Why, he even makes the hairs on the back of their necks stand tall," Smith mentioned.

"So what can we do?" Williams inquired.

"Somebody needs to play a good trick on him. I hear he doesn't get along with Lt. Carlton."

"So?" Williams asked.

"All someone has to do is sneak into Lt. Carlton's BOQ and leave a calling card. After that just sit back and watch the fireworks." Smith grinned from ear to ear.

"But who? And what kind of calling card?"

Smith leaned over on his bunk. "I hear Lt. Carlton lives near a farmhouse where a farmer raises all kinds of chickens and roosters. They wake him very early in the morning."

Williams shrugged his shoulders. "And?"

"Don't you get it? He hates roosters. We could get someone in our outfit to plant a rooster in his BOQ with Sgt. Lambert's calling card. Then bingo. That drill sergeant will be history after Lt. Carlton sinks his teeth into him."

"You've still got to find someone who hates Lambert more than us," Williams interjected.

Mike watched as the two privates looked in his direction. He continued polishing his boots. They stepped over then sat down on his bunk.

"We can count you in, can't we Fairmont?" Smith asked.

"Me?" Mike swallowed with a loud gulp.

"Yeah. The man really gets under your skin. You of all people should want to make his life as miserable as he has made yours," Williams said.

Again Mike swallowed. "Sure. But what about my career?"

"What career? We've only been here for three weeks. What can they possibly do to you? Throw you out of the Army?"

Mike felt a gleam his eye. Now wouldn't that be nice? But still.

"Fairmont, I don't like that look. You aren't chicken are you?" Smith asked.

"Why does it have to be me? There are others in this outfit who dislike him."

"But you're the one he continues to trample on. It should be you," Smith replied.

"Where am I going to get a rooster?"

"Leave that up to us," Smith said.

That had been one experience that Mike would end up telling his grandchildren about. That is, if he lived through the ordeal by the time the lieutenant and the drill sergeant got through with him.

Now he sat in Lt. Carlton's office waiting to hear the verdict that would affect his career. He had once again been stupid enough to listen to someone else pull him into another web. This time it hadn't been any recruiting officer. It had been Smith and Williams. They had set him up big time. He had been their butt of all jokes.

When the door flew open, Mike stood at attention. Lt. Carlton walked in with Sgt. Lambert.

"At ease, Fairmont. Sit back down," Lt. Carlton said.

Mike stood stiff like someone had put too much starch in his fatigues.

"It's all right. Sit down. Be comfortable," Lt. Carlton issued.

Lt. Carlton sat down behind his desk. Sgt. Lambert pulled up a chair beside Mike. It was so quiet in the room, you could hear a pin drop.

"Sgt. Lambert and I have discussed this. And we have finally come up with a decision."

"Sir, if I may speak," Mike started slowly. "I truly am sorry. I had no business listening to Pvt. Smith and Williams. In fact, I had no business listening to the Army Recruiting Officer. I was stupid to join the Army."

"That's where Sgt. Lambert and I draw the line."

"Excuse me, sir?"

Sgt. Lambert got up from his chair. "Fairmont, do you wanna know the real reason I pick on you?"

Mike eyed him, curious.

"You remind me of myself when I was your age. I was a naive young boy fresh out of high school when I joined the Army. Believe me, it was somewhat different in my time than it is for the ones joining today. My drill sergeant pounded me like a nail. You see, he saw potential in this skinny young kid. Just like I saw in you when you stepped off that bus. You can't go through life allowing others to pick on you. There comes a time when you must take a stand. But placing a rooster in Lt. Carlton's BOQ wasn't the answer."

"Especially with the mess that red-headed monster made. Placing some of my uniforms on the floor for him to do his little chicken mess on wasn't such a bright treat either. In fact, he wrecked havoc on a lot of my items. The smell was something that I hadn't anticipated," Lt. Carlton said.

"Sir, I'm willing to make amends for any damages. You can have my whole paycheck plus, if necessary. When Smith and Williams mentioned this might get me out of the Army, I agreed to take the plunge. But now, I feel like a stupid school-boy. My aunt and uncle would truly be disappointed in my actions. I'm not too proud of myself at this point. It certainly wasn't a smart move on my career. Are you and Sgt. Lambert going to court-martial me?"

"Is that what you want?" Lt. Carlton inquired.

"No, sir. I would like another chance."

"You realize your training is still going to be rough before it gets better. We have to mold boys into men if we want this country on solid ground. Sgt. Lambert takes his job task serious."

"Yes, sir." Mike took a pause, inhaling a breath. "Sgt. Lambert, again I apologize for my actions."

"To err is human, Fairmont. And all of us at one time or another make some mistakes in our lives. As for the damages—"

"Yes, the damages," Lt. Carlton interrupted. "That billing will be sent to the two who initiated this whole ploy. I think as you progress in your training that you'll find others will seek to use you as their guinea pig in their attacks. Don't let that happen. You are too smart for those tactics."

"I've learned my lesson."

"That, I'm glad to hear. After Sgt. Lambert and I get a hold of Smith and Williams, we'll see who really gets the last laugh. Don't worry. Sgt. Lambert and I are going to make sure they know you had no part in us finding out they were behind this. We have our ways."

"Sir, if I may ask, why are you and Sgt. Lambert not being so harsh with me?"

Lt. Carlton shot Sgt. Lambert a smile. "I guess you could say I was in the same boat as Sgt. Lambert when I entered the

Army. After being picked on all my life in school, I vowed after joining the Army, I'd never let others cast another stone at me. Guess you could say us birds of a feather truly do stick together. Now you march out there and become a good soldier before we change our minds."

"Who knows, Fairmont," Sgt. Lambert said. "After you finish your basic here and go on to greener pastures, you might end up returning to Ft. Benning to become a drill sergeant yourself. Then you could give some of the men a run for their money, too. See the potential in others, as I have seen in you."

Mike quickly stood at attention. "Yes, sir, Lt. Carlton, Sgt. Lambert. One never knows what journeys our life will carry us on." He saluted them both before leaving the room.

By the time his feet hit the pavement outside, his nervous stomach had abated. The weight had finally been lifted from his shoulders. He was one young soldier who wasn't smuggling anything else into anyone's BOQ. There would be no more crossing into another's boundaries. From now on, it would be smooth sailing. He was determined to become the best soldier the United States Army had seen in a long time.

Let's go South for the Winter
A New Journey

Being enlisted in the armed forces, a young man or woman finds many places to travel and see. The old saying for many in the Navy would ring, *join the Navy and see the world, but what did we see, but the sea.* Mike Fairmont wasn't Navy bound; rather he had chosen the Army. Bryan had opted for the Air Force, while his other two brothers went into different fields, civilian instead of military. Their aging years still didn't bring them closer together, only farther in distance.

Throughout each of their wandering journeys, he would have to say Bryan was the only one he stayed in touch with or visited. His other brothers had only twice sprung an occasional unexpected visit on him. After his mother's passing, they were seldom seen. As everyone began getting older and having their own families, no one really had the time to visit, or even communicate with one another. As for Mike Fairmont, after he sailed past his twenty-first birthday, he was a man on his own.

This was his second time at Ft. Benning, Georgia. The year of 1968 was about to show a twist of events for the young man, who had recently turned twenty-three. His work had been his main interest in life as he plunged headlong into the military life.

While Bryan sought the Air Force, then altered his course for the Army, seeking Officer Candidate School, Mike chose to stay an enlisted man.

The people of the south did speak with a slightly different dialect than the northerners, but he soon found himself fitting snugly into their lifestyle. It was totally different from where he had been raised, but he enjoyed the *southern hospitality,* as others plainly referred to it. The first time he had visited Ft. Benning was during his basic training. He was a young man at that time. He recalled the rooster incident. A memory that would always stay branded in his memory. It was a time in his journey that led him in the pathway of maturity.

Before leaving the state of Ohio, he had found a young woman he cared about. He had told his heart that he would never get serious with anyone after Brenda but he had found someone out there. Even though he had strong feelings for her, they had yet to set plans for a marriage. Carol Talmet was her name, and she was more mature than his last girlfriend had been.

She was enlisting into the Air Force, and for her, the number one thing in her life at the moment was her job. Mike, too, carried the same thoughts. They were sure their love for one another was strong enough to withstand any distance apart. Their relationship was not that of an official engagement, so they were free to date other people. This was one way of finding out for sure if they were indeed meant for one another.

The best thing he loved about the south was the weather. He had grown tired of the snow and freezing temperatures of the north. His bones were arriving at a stage in his life that they no longer would stay warm. The warmer temperatures of the south were a welcome change he highly favored. One change that was not pleasant, however, was the new troops that he had to break in.

He was now a drill sergeant and drilling the new NOTC students was a job and a half. He understood what his first drill sergeant underwent day in and out. Many of these new recruits acted like dumb goof balls. He was curious how they ever were allowed entry into the Army. Another slight change he resented was the First Sergeant over him. He was his own man and always had dreaded someone else having the rule over him. This new First Sergeant was just that. Mike found him to be a lot more difficult than the drill sergeant during his basic training many years prior.

Mike saw the First Sergeant as a hard man who didn't take kindly to constructive criticism or like to be wrong in any situation. For Mike, this was going to be an uphill climb for the both of them. What they didn't see in the mirror before them was the fact that they were identical in their own separate ways, but neither one would ever tell the other.

Throughout all the years they would eventually share, there would be resentment, hatred, bitter words, negativity and the constant battle as to who would rule or be dominent in their world. They would later, down the road, share a good many talks and sorrows together, but each of the two would always think he knew more than the other did. If one was right, neither would ever admit it. The constant battle would escalate, but only one would end up winning and really revealing his love and admiration to the other.

Yes, as Mike eyed the First Sergeant he considered austere, he was unaware the man behind the stripes would within the year be his father-in-law.

Love at First Sight
The First Sergeant's Daughter

She had no idea what was drawing her to the man in the blue suit, but for some unforeseen reason, she felt as if a magnet were pulling her into his web. The first thing that she noticed was his eyes. Dreamy, full eyes that popped out at you. Eyes that absorbed you like a sponge, drinking all of you in. That was the man who would be her husband, the man she would marry and have children with. He was unaware because they had yet to really be introduced, but yes, he was the man of her long awaited dreams.

Her dad didn't know when he took the family to the dinner for the captain of his outfit that his seventeen-year-old daughter would fall head over heels in love with the man who irritated him endlessly with every passing day. The only words he said about the man were, "That is Sgt. Fairmont He enjoys running my blood pressure up every morning."

The more her daddy mentioned the man, the more she had to learn about him. She would never tell her father though. In his military handbook, he would choose whom his daughters would date and marry. As for her, even at seventeen, she had yet to even be on a date. All she knew was the Army life, and she figured until her death an Army brat was what she would stay. But that was before she met the dashing, handsome Mike Fairmont. The one man who could melt her heart with his eyes, and break it in two if he ever got the chance. There was no way to warn her he had another woman in the wings, and even though they had made no plans to seriously marry, Carol carried his heart close within her bosom. But one thing Carol didn't know was once Bonnie got her hooks on Mike; her love for him would be so deep that she would never see him as harming even a gnat.

Two months after the captain's dinner party, Mike happened to run into Bonnie. He had rented a house very near where she and her parents lived. This didn't make the First Sergeant a happy man, but he wasn't the landlord, so he had no choice in the matter.

She was a southern lady, with values, so she acted accordingly. He was the first to speak and extent his hand in friendship.

"Hi, my name is Mike Fairmont. Didn't I see you at the captain's dinner party a while back?"

"Yes, two months ago, to be exact." She had marked the date on her calendar, circling it with red ink. It had been a night she would never forget.

"You sat at the table with my First Sergeant...don't tell me you're his daughter?"

"Yes."

He stared at the dark auburn hair, blue eyes and dimples that showed when she smiled.

"What?" she asked, smiling as he continued to stare.

"Excuse me?"

"You're practically putting holes in me with your eyes."

He laughed. "Sorry, I was trying to figure out the resemblance. But I just remembered he hasn't much hair, so it's hard to really place you as his daughter."

"I favor my mother."

"Yes, that resemblance I can see."

"I see you're moving in. Do you need any help?"

"Not at the moment. I have a buddy from base who is helping. He is going to be sharing the rent with me."

"Well, I guess I'll leave you to get settled. If you need any help, give me a call. I'll be more than glad to help."

"Thanks, I'll keep that in mind," he said, with a wink of his eye.

She was almost certain he had seen her blushing. The rush of heat was rising, sending tiny bubbles similar to champagne fizz throughout her veins as she walked briskly back to her house.

She wrote all her inner secrets down in a book, and kept it under lock and key. One thing she didn't need was her brothers getting hold of the diary and repeating each sentence to her daddy. No, that wouldn't benefit her at all.

There were only a few months left of school, and graduation would be upon her. She made a habit of walking past Mike's house every other day, especially after school. She had met his buddy, Randall Midfield. He was tall, muscular, with rich jet-black hair, and two years younger than Mike, whereas Mike was not too tall, had green eyes and didn't look to be muscular in any way. He didn't seem to be the type that would really draw women, but Bonnie thought otherwise. She thought Mike to be a very handsome man in his own way.

As for her best friend, she thought of all the people to fall in love with, why not Randall? After all, he was by far the better looking and the easiest to get along with. But Bonnie wasn't in love with Randall, as she quickly let Alice know, mentioning that if she thought him to be so outstanding, why didn't she go after him? Alice replied hastily with a "I just might," as she smacked her gum.

Randall was the one who ended up bringing Mike and Bonnie together. She had secured his trust as she explained how much she was in love with Mike. Randall told her everything was in complete confidence, but what she didn't know was after he drank a few too many beers, his tongue ran loose to anyone next to him. Without thinking, he confessed all of Bonnie's secrets to Mike.

Sure it was the beer in his system, Mike was stupefied at the announcement. The next morning when he was sober, he would question Randall's words.

Feeling like a heel for breaking Bonnie's trust, Randall confessed it to be the gospel truth. Back home, Mike and Carol had said they would date others during their separation, but he hadn't dated anyone since arriving in Georgia. Now, to be told the First Sergeant's daughter was head over heels in love with him, he was fairly sure the old man didn't know, or he would have been on a slow boat to China by now.

Randall made him promise not to let Bonnie know the words had slipped out during a night of too many beers. Mike had promised. He took a walk after hearing of the new development in his life, wondering how to act upon it and even if he should. He liked Bonnie, but she was still a high school girl. She would be graduating soon and probably had plans to enter some college or stay single the rest of her life. No, that wouldn't be the case, if she cared for him the way Randall described, all her future plans would be forsaken to marry a man like Mike Fairmont.

He beamed excitedly. Never had any young girl fallen head over heels for him in that way. Perhaps his luck was about to change for the better. Maybe he would invite her out to a movie or dinner...perhaps. Surely her dad wouldn't disagree to a simple date.

In the beginning, Bonnie's dad was furious when he heard Sgt. Fairmont wished to take his daughter out. *No way!* he had barked. His daughter had never been out on a date and her first would not be with a philandering sergeant, especially someone much older than her.

Bonnie's mother was somewhat more sympathetic and talked to her husband. After all, Bonnie was seventeen and soon to be out of school, just what harm would it be? The discussion went on for a day and a half, before her dad finally came around. She could go, but he had better have her back by midnight...and not one minute later.

Boy, was this going to be a fun night or what, she wondered. The pressure was so intense, how would they even enjoy their meal or a movie? Laying all differences aside, they concentrated on the night. Everything else didn't exist.

Bonnie was ecstatic with the touch of his hand, or the look in his eyes. They were so hypnotic, captivating. She had never known love, but what she was feeling; she knew it had to be the real thing.

Days passed and there were other dates, other moments to share, and then the kiss she had long awaited. Fireworks exploded and her insides melted like butter when his lips touched hers and locked into a kiss. His hand hugged the inner portion of her back as he pulled her closer to his warmth. She was sure her body would rupture soon. The explosion would be so loud that everyone in the area would hear her squeal with rapture.

When the kissing stopped, he looked deep into her eyes, searching for her inner soul. Was this the girl that he could share his life with? The one that would be his friend, his lover, his confidant—the backbone of strength, like his mother?

She smiled and half nodded her head, bewildered by his sharp attentive stare. He was a strange man to even try to figure out, so she chose to leave some things unmentioned.

The next day, he withdrew Bonnie from classes early and took her to lunch. As she started to take a bite of her salad, she observed a shining object centered next to the tomato wedge.

"What is this? I could break a tooth," she causally said.

After a closer look at it, then seeing Mike's shy smile, she bolted from her seat and raced over to him, hugging and kissing him in front of the whole restaurant.

"Well, will you marry me, Bonnie Wilcox?"

"What took you so long in asking, Sgt. Fairmont?"

He reached for the ring and slid it on her finger. Their eyes made contact as his lips joined hers in a loving kiss.

"How did you even know my ring size?"

"I'm a Sergeant. I do have my ways," he said with a wink of the eye.

Bonnie gave him a warm smile. She was finally going to wed the man she had fallen in love with at first sight, while he had found the one perfect mate to lift all his troubled spirits. For now all the bad memories of the past would stay buried. This was a new step for him. One he was certain would be filled with wonderful journeys.

The Misunderstanding
Newlyweds

"Nobody does that to me and gets away with it," Bonnie huffed as she made her way to the door.

"Bonnie, hold up a minute."

She turned and gave Mike a cold stare, then placed her hands on her hips. "For what? We've only been married for five months. All I hear is the Army this or the Army that. I've had it up to my neck with the Army."

"Whoa, wait up. When we married, didn't you know I was in the Army?"

"Yes, but—"

"No buts about anything. Not only that, you knew what kind of life came along being an Army wife. After all, your dad was in the military when I first met you. All those years of being in the military, you had some idea what would be taking place after we said our marriage vows."

She started to answer but he didn't allow her.

"Granted you were only seventeen when we married, but I was sure that you would be mature enough to understand my extra duty at times. I'm sorry that I can't spend every waking moment with you, Bonnie, but I do have a job to perform everyday. I know we don't have much time of late to spend with each other with all the new troops pouring into the base for their basic training, but have you forgotten there is a war going on?"

No, she had not forgotten anything about that dreaded war, something that Mike knew was worrying her every night when they kissed one another as they prepared for bed. Every time they turned on the radio or television, news of the fighting overseas bombarded them. He had heard Bonnie tossing and turning in her sleep many a night since they married. He had assured her that he had already been over there once. Surely they wouldn't send him again. But with the Army anything could happen, as he found out months down the road.

"I know in time things will be better for the both of us, sweetheart," he said, trying to console her. She was so young and pretty standing near the door with her hands flattened on her hips. At times he still couldn't believe that her father had approved of their marriage, but he had.

Bonnie had wanted to go off and get married. Mike said no. He wanted to see his new bride wearing a white dress as she floated down the aisle. He wanted them both to be able to walk under the drawn swords as the soldiers gathered in a row for their departure once they were pronounced husband and wife. He had received his wish and he wouldn't have changed it for the world.

Bonnie kept her hands on her hips then tapped her foot. She wondered what that look on his face implied. After five months, he was still as handsome as the day that he said I do, but this time she wasn't going to allow him to win. She understood what military life involved, but face it, military men had families just like the next person. They needed time to be with their wives, especially with the thought of the husband having to go overseas to fight the enemy.

She immediately shook that thought away. She didn't want to have to see her husband go flying off to fight in a foreign land. She wanted him to stay with her, love her and make babies with her. She wanted that perfect family that she had always dreamed of. She didn't want to lose him in a foreign land.

Mike saw that intense stare lingering in her eyes. The one that he had grown accustomed to since they had been introduced. No, Bonnie had to listen this time. This was his career. He had made it such before he made the agreement of marriage with her. She understood this from the beginning and accepted it.

"You can blow all the smoke you want but it's not going to help matters. I plan to make the Army my life-long career as well as our marriage a life-long commitment. Now that I'm up for a promotion with another stripe, you want to up and jump ship."

"Do you blame me? We're still on our honeymoon."

"I can't help it; the door blew open for me. Not only that, it will mean more money for us. We can always use that extra income. Down the road we will want to have children. If I recall, you wanted ten, and I wanted nine. Of course I do believe that we will end up changing our minds and have three or four children at the most."

"You think?" she said, not flinching.

"Yes, I do."

"I'm not happy with these new surroundings, Mike. I didn't know that your job was going to take preference over me. I don't appreciate your actions. I, for one, won't allow it!"

Mike struck the top of his head. "Haven't you heard one word I've said? This is my job. I'm not allowing it to put you on the back burner. I have to think about a roof over your head and food on the table, Bonnie. I am doing this for the both of us. Our future together as husband and wife. I promised not only you, but your parents that I would take care of you until death us do part."

"And I'm your wife. I want my husband with me always. Not just for a passing moment."

"In other words, we can live off of love?"

"Oh, Michael!"

"Well that is what your words are implying. I don't understand you. In fact I've never seen you this way. You are different from the woman I married five months ago. And I know you are not going through any menopause. You're way too young for that. This cuts deeper. Not only that, I hear you at night tossing and turning as you sleep. You are worried about this war, Bonnie. I hate to say this but perhaps you should go speak to your mother."

That had not hit the spot with Bonnie. She glared at him.

"If you must know, I'm worried about not spending any time with my dear husband anymore. His job and his trainees take up all his days and nights." She cast him another angry look then raced out the door.

Mike shook his head then changed into his fatigues. He had to go to work just like anyone else who held a job. He couldn't call out, and especially not in the military. He didn't understand Bonnie's behavior. She was a military brat. What could have happened in the last five months to change her attitude about their marriage?

Later that night, Bonnie grilled a couple of steaks, baked

a couple of potatoes and tossed a green salad. She waited for Mike's car to pull into the driveway before turning off the lights.

"Bonnie, did we forget to pay the electric bill?" Mike asked, stumbling into the house and trying to find the light switch.

"Of course not, silly."

"Then why the candles?"

"As if you didn't know? I'm trying to make amends. I was very abrupt earlier today. Now don't bother flipping that light switch on or I'll turn it right back off. Notice that I'm even wearing your favorite nightgown?"

"I noticed. What's that I smell? Steak?"

"Yes, I prepared it just the way you like it. After I left here, I went to the commissary and got a few items."

He sniffed. "It does smell great. Does it come with a baked potato and salad?" Mike asked.

"You bet."

"And for dessert?" he asked with raised eyebrows.

"Why do you think I'm wearing the nightgown you bought me?"

Mike smiled. "I say we go for the dessert first."

"You wicked drill sergeant," she said as he embraced her warmly.

It had been a night that had brought them closer together in more ways than one.

The week ahead proved to be smooth sailing. Bonnie seemed more at ease with the situation. She had thought the matter over and decided she had been a bit unfair to Mike. Their marriage vows carried a lot of clout. She didn't wish to lose the man she loved more than anything. He had been correct about her ability to understand, being a military brat herself. She had decided to rethink the matter and be the supporting wife that he had married.

"What are you looking at, Mike?" Bonnie said one evening when she noticed him watching her.

"You. I can't get over how you've changed this past week. You're humming a whole different tune."

"I'm trying to be that understanding military wife I so often hear about. I didn't want another one of our misunderstandings to end in divorce. And you were right, a military brat should understand fully in these situations."

Mike frowned.

"Mike, don't worry about the divorce thing. I'd never divorce you. I just want you to remember even though you're married to the Army, you still have a wife."

"That I could never forget." He rubbed the back of his neck.

"Now you're sporting another look, sweetheart. I don't think I like this one."

Mike issued a breath. "This week I'm going to be extremely busy with my studying, not to mention drilling all those new recruits. Everything has to be hush-hush quiet. I have to leave before the crack of dawn. And some nights I may have to stay later to prepare for the next day."

"So I'm a war widow once more."

"I wouldn't go that far. I'll at least be with you at night when we're in bed."

Bonnie rolled her eyes. "I suppose I can spend my time silently reading or knitting."

"That's my girl." *Knitting.* "Wait a minute, when did you take up knitting? You don't even care for sewing."

"Just to coin a phrase, Mike. I'll bide my time doing something constructive."

Mike spent his hours cramming. Bonnie bided her time the best she knew how. Most of the time she read through new cookbooks, learning new recipes to try. Other times she would read a good book, making a nice little collection in the den where she kept her books. Or spend some time visiting friends or her mom. Every day she continued looking for that silver lining. Surely, once the school was completed with the new recruits, Mike would have more free time to spend with her.

Three days before the last training day, Bonnie grew nervous and irritable. She wasn't feeling well. Hadn't been feeling well for some time now. She decided to make an appointment on base to see a doctor. One thing was certain; she was tired of being a widow.

The next day, Mike dragged in around five. Bonnie had the table all set. Maybe tonight he would be up to a little romance. He had been cramming too hard lately, not only with the books he had to study at home but with his job on base as well. She hadn't informed him of her doctor visit yet. She thought she should tell him before she forgot.

"What happened to my kiss?" Bonnie asked.

"Honey, I gave you one," Mike answered in a tired voice.

"More like a chicken peck, if you ask me."

"Bonnie, please, no sarcasm tonight. I'm really beat. My brain is worn out from storing so much data. Not to mention my feet sore from so much marching with those troops these past few days."

"Excuse me. I thought tonight we could have had one night together."

"Bonnie, please don't start in on the Army stuff again. This is really hard on me. I'm not willing to become a failure."

"Sorry. Guess I was being a little short-tempered again. I miss your closeness. Why don't you eat? Then we can turn in together?" She questioned within herself now, should she even tell him about the visit to the doctor?

"I'm not hungry. I've got to be in at eight in the morning. If I go on to bed now, I can get plenty of sleep. Would you mind setting the clock for me? I'm changing clothes, then I'm out for the night."

Bonnie quietly wrapped the meal. It would keep till the next day. When she went to set the clock alarm, Mike was out like a light. When she reached for the alarm clock, a brilliant thought raced through her mind. She smiled wickedly.

At seven, the alarm began buzzing. Mike jumped out of bed and started dressing. He yawned. Bonnie was sitting on the edge of the bed.

"Oh, honey. You didn't have to wake up. I wanted you to sleep in. I don't even feel like I got any sleep. It seems like no sooner did I get into dreamland then that stupid buzzer went off."

Bonnie cupped her mouth. She tried to refrain from laughing. Yawning, Mike slipped on his pants and gave her a strange look.

"Boy, am I tired. I'll probably fall asleep in class. That's going to really look great."

Bonnie broke out in laughter. Mike wondered why the loud outburst. "Are you all right?"

She nodded, still laughing uncontrollably.

"Come on, Bonnie. Let me in on the funny joke."

She tried to speak through the laughter. "Promise you

won't be mad?"

Mike crossed his arms. "What have you done?" He looked out the window blind. Then eyed the clock. "Bonnie? You better come clean with me."

She fell off the bed, rolling in laughter. She started speaking but Mike couldn't understand her. He walked over to the clock and checked the buzzer.

"You little witch. You set the clock to go off at seven p.m. instead of a.m. No wonder I still feel tired. Were you going to allow me go on out to the car? Then tell me?"

Bonnie wiped the wetness from her face as tears of joy ran down her cheeks. She held tight to her stomach. The laughter had really become uncontrollable.

"Really amusing, Bonnie."

"I was tired of being an Army widow. I thought it was funny."

Mike snickered. "It showed."

"Are you mad?"

He looked at the clock, then Bonnie. He, too, broke out in laughter. "I think this is the best misunderstanding we've ever had."

"So I'm forgiven?"

"I'll get you back."

"Promises, promises," she said as they rolled in laughter together.

"Here I thought my body was ready for a total meltdown. I mean I knew something was wrong. I didn't feel like I had gotten any rest."

"Again, I am so sorry, sweetheart. I had wanted to tell you about my visit to the doctor yesterday. This was my chance tonight and you were so eager to run off to bed."

"I was exhausted, Bonnie." He shook his head. "Wait a minute. You went to the doctor without me knowing anything about it. What's wrong?"

"I haven't been feeling myself lately. I was able to get in on post yesterday afternoon."

He opened his hands. "Well, are you going to tell me what's wrong? I mean, everything is all right?"

"Yes, Mike, honey, everything is fine."

"Well, next time you let me know when you have to go to the doctor for anything." He kissed her on the cheek then began slipping out of his clothes. "Now I do have to get some rest before morning. And no more hanky panky, you hear me?"

She smiled wide.

"I mean it, Bonnie Fairmont."

"Scouts honor."

"I'll make it all up to you in just a couple more days."

"I'll keep you to your word, Mike. Oh, one more thing, you will need to mark on your calendar a month from today. I have to go back to the doctor then. And you told me to let you know when I need to go."

He rolled to his side. "I thought you said you were okay."

"Oh, I am Mike. I just have to see a doctor for the next seven months since I'm pregnant."

Mike's eyes grew wide as he jumped out of the bed.

"Did I hear you right?" he asked, clutching her hand.

"Yes, seems most of my moodiness is due to pregnancy. Can you believe that?"

Mike grinned. He was going to be a father. Have his own little Mike or Bonnie running around the house. How lucky could a man get? This was a day that would go down in history in his book.

He recalled the beginning of his journey. A journey that was made the moment he left his mother's womb and made a pathway into the huge world that awaited him. So much had happened during that time until now.

He took Bonnie in his arms and held her tightly before he feathered her with kisses. Then he pulled her onto the bed with him as they held onto each other. They thought of names for boys and girls, then once again proclaimed their love for each other. It was a night filled with pleasant talk and moments that neither of them would ever forget.

They only wanted to think of happy occasions, not of any war across the ocean. Nor about what lay in the future for them. They only saw tonight in their future and the important news of bringing a baby into the world. As they cuddled in each other's arms, neither anticipated the possibility of Mike not being there for the birth of his first child. Nor how Bonnie would be bedridden in her sixth month due to the baby already dropping so early. Neither even considered that the war that was moving with great speed would call Mike to have to transfer to a land that was filling fast with blood and tears. All they thought about was the blessed moment that they were now sharing with each other. Everything else was placed on the back burner.

Journeys from a Boy to a Man
The Dreaded War...Missing Families

The dark coldness of the night, from the earlier falling of the monsoon rain, had indeed left a chill on the young men. Not only had the drop in temperature affected them, but also the possibility of an enemy advancement sent chills of fear throughout the young men's spines.

No one knew if the foxholes they had hidden in during the nights would keep them safe from harm.

Sgt. Mike Fairmont was leader of his platoon. It was up to him to be strong for his troops, not allowing any sense of dread or fright to creep into his vocabulary. If the men suspected him to be a coward, no doubt they would hightail it back away from the front lines.

The man stood only five-feet-eight inches, with around one hundred fifty-five pounds on his medium frame. All through his life he had been short for a man, and was considered to be of a puny stature. He often thought of King David in the Old Testament Bible when he eyed himself in nature. After having to overcome so many obstacles, he hoped that with the help of the Lord he would be able to get through any conflict in his wanderings about the earth.

The only sound that could be heard in the Viet Cong jun-

gle's outback was a few noises of insects. The bites of the insects alone were enough to drive a man to react to every little
sound. The huge mosquito had to be watched due to the large
outbreak of malaria.

The sudden sound of tree branches bending and snapping
produced a few scary noises, and the men wondered if perhaps an enemy had quietly entered their mist. Mike soon once
more discovered in his overseas journey to a land of bombing
and fighting that there were other causes of death besides illness or car accidents or other fatal catastrophes.

He had hoped to be free from this dreaded ordeal of going to war, but being in the military, when duty called, he
didn't disobey any orders. As he caught a glimpse of the other
men in his outfit, he saw faces bearing expressions of sadness,
fright, worry. Everyone in his outfit had a loved one back
home, whether parents, wife, sister or grandparents, they
each had a particular person waiting back in the states for their
return. None of them knew who would live or who would
die—all of that didn't rest in their hands.

Many offered prayers that the Vietnam crisis would soon
be over, while others were eager to blow heads off the enemy.

He, on the other hand, wanted no war, only peace. The
people they were fighting had families, too. Before all of it
was over there would be many a life lost, and many a soldier
wounded. Talk of soldiers already taken prisoner was rapidly
passing through the camp. So many of the young admitted
they'd rather die than be captured as a prisoner of war and be
tortured.

As he continued to look around the setting of the camp,
only he and the others, who had to face such a conflict, knew

what was going on around them. The others back home protesting or waiting for the arrival of returned family knew nothing of what these young boys and grown men had to endure in this dreadful war. Half of them would either be dead and sent back home in a body bag, while the others would mature at an early age as they faced the land of tears and sorrow.

His eyes closed for a moment as he thought of home. Oh, how he wished he could be there in her arms, holding her tightly next to his chest. He had married the young Bonnie Wilcox after her high school graduation. Her father had not been too keen on the idea. Being Mike's First Sergeant, he disliked the man with a passion; of course, at times, the feeling was mutual for Mike.

Bonnie so often would concede that they couldn't get along because the two of them were so much alike, always wanting to be right over every situation.

After some persuasion from Bonnie's mother, her father had agreed to a wedding, only if that was what his daughter really wanted. It truly was, more than anything.

He opened his eyes and pulled his wallet out of his fatigue pocket. He carried her picture with him everywhere he went, never wanting to part with her beauty. When he received his orders for Vietnam, she was already seven months pregnant with their first child. It had been painful for him to leave her, but he had no choice. For the first time since his own mother's death, when he was but a small boy of ten, he had cried.

Bonnie had filled an void in the deepest, darkest hours of his life. He was saddened that his firstborn would be born while he was away from her side. Bonnie's parents would be with her, but all of that wouldn't be the same. Together they had conceived that little bundle she was carrying. He should have been there to share the impending joy of birth. He didn't know once they were pronounced man and wife that his journey in life would again take him to this dark dismal jungle. He thought there would never be any more sadness in his life.

There was one last look at her picture, then a kiss on the small portrait before he put it back into his wallet. He remembered her daddy wasn't the only one that had wanted to stir up a hassle over his marriage to Bonnie.

Carol Talmet, his old girlfriend from Ohio, had tried her best to break up their engagement. She would phone long distance, insisting he was promised to her and her only. When that little ploy didn't work, she even enlisted the aid of her good friend's help. She figured if her good friend phoned Mike to inform him that Carol had been badly injured in an automobile wreck, he would certainly come rushing to her side. Wrong, dead wrong. In no time, he figured all the manipulating procedures were only a way of messing with his mind, but it didn't work. He never fell victim to any of her schemes.

The wedding held in the chapel, with the soldiers holding the swords as they walked under them hand in hand, had indeed been the most beautiful event he had ever participated in.

A loud sound of a gun being fired off in a distance alarmed him. He jumped and looked around. It wasn't near his outfit though. Rather, it was miles from them, but the second sound of the machine gun seemed so very close, as if thunder was ripping in and out of the valley.

He sat back in the groove, in the dirt that had held his body. Taking a deep breath, he inhaled what he thought was clean air, but it reeked of death. The smell of blood on young men's flesh—whether American or Viet Cong—would still be red. The pain of death would still be felt by any race at war. Embittered hearts would continue to experience pain until some form of relief could be sought.

Inside he was scared, but he would never permit his soldiers to even see these traits reflecting on his countenance. That wouldn't be proper for another soldier higher in command to permit others to perceive him as a possible failure or coward. With a bite of his lip, he silently prayed, hoping that soon this plight would be over, and that the lives of these young men of whatever nationality, fighting for whatever cause, would be spared at all costs. With the final word spoken, he tried to catch any sleep that the silence of the dark night would allow.

* * * *

Mail call was a most welcome event for the soldiers, even for those who didn't receive mail; the others shared the news of home with them. Mike would request boxes of canned food, box cakes, and homemade cookies from Bonnie. He was growing weary of Army rations, which had absolutely no taste. Bonnie's goodies she sent him made a slight dent in their money budget, but boosted his morale considerably.

When the packages didn't come, he would be swamped with letters and pictures of home. Bonnie had given birth to a beautiful baby girl and he wanted oodles of snapshots of his baby daughter, Victoria. A name that fitted the baby like a glove to a hand. It was definitely becoming to their princess. A tear fell from his eye when he first saw the little tot. Even more so, as mother stood holding the child in her arms. It was through the Red Cross that he had learned of her birth, wishing immensely that he could have been there for the delivery. The news had been exciting, but he would have much rather heard it first hand from his wife, still the young nurse from the Red Cross facilities had been extremely cordial.

He recalled how he had to say goodbye to her when he left for the war. Neither wanted the separation but it was part of life in his job and they both had to accept that. He didn't want to leave her alone and pregnant. He knew her parents were there, but he wanted to be the one watching over her, especially when the doctor said after the sixth month she needed bed rest so the baby would not drop anymore.

There had been some nights when he had cooked for her, and when he handed her the plate of food, she'd always smiled and remarked about how thoughtful he was. Nevertheless, she hated being confined to either a chair or a bed. But when the doctor said not to even lift a broom, Mike had instructed her it was the doctor's orders. He smiled as he thought of the time he presented her with pork chops, mashed potatoes, and applesauce. She grew curious as to what was sprinkled atop her applesauce. When he said cinnamon, her smile turned to a frown, but she had eaten it. She did suggest no more cinnamon on her applesauce. That was an evening he would always remember as well.

His thoughts roamed to the moments after his own birth when he had first been placed in his mother's arms. And she had cherished him until her death. Oh, there was that word again, *death.* He seemed to dwell more on it lately than ever before. He didn't want to leave his wife a widow, no, not now, not ever. He had to live to return home, hold her in his arms again, and hug the new life they had brought into the world. There were only ten months left for him in this jungle.

He was certain the prayers would come even more frequent now.

Not long after baby Victoria's birth, there had been a torrential rain in the jungle once again. This time it was accompanied with lightening. With no place to run for shelter except under the branch of a huge Vietnamese tree—one Mike didn't really know the name of—he ran to the tree and stood beneath it until the huge raindrops slackened. When the shower was almost over, he heard a loud pop as thunder rumbled and realized he'd been struck in his arm.

He recalled falling to the ground and lying in silence as others came rushing to his rescue. Four of the young soldiers carefully picked him up and carried him to his tent, placing him on his bunk. Another ran to get the medic on call.

The lightning had struck him in the arm, almost paralyzing his body, but he had been fortunate because the symptom only lingered for twenty-four hours. Then he was back to himself. He said a prayer of thanks to his Maker above. He was more than glad he had been spared. This incident would not be reported to Bonnie for fear of worrying her. If he lived to return home, he would tell her of his ordeal with the lightening bolt, but not before. She had enough to worry about with this dreadful war.

As the months seemed to roll along, his thoughts were always with his wife and baby daughter, but only when he didn't foresee any danger from the enemy. There was another brush with death when a mosquito bite infected him with malaria. This was not reported to Bonnie either; at least not until he returned home. His siege with malaria was by far the closest that Mike had come to dying. The whole ordeal had been a miserable time in his life. The lonely hours he lay feverish in the hospital brought recurring nightmares. The insect bite alone caused his body to go through so much that he felt as if he were already dying. He hoped that he would never have to endure such a terrible ordeal ever again. At this early stage in time, he would never know it would stay with him, even later in life.

As his day to finally return to his homeland quickly approached, Mike was relieved that his days in the war were rapidly drawing to a close. The anticipation at times was hard to cope with. He was sure all of the last days were just as intense for Bonnie.

The day of departure was a sad one for Mike. It was another turning point in his life as he told his brave soldiers goodbye. He told them that if there was any way he could take them back with him, he would, but that truly was an impossible dream. His prayers and thoughts would stay with them, as he always carried their memory embedded within his heart. With a fond farewell of a wave and salute, he left his young, brave soldiers. There was a big bird that he had to board that would fly him to his homeland.

Mike grew weary at the delays, holdovers, and changing of the planes. On the other side of the world waited his wife and new daughter. He wanted a non-stop flight, but at the time that was asking too much. He would have to settle for a few more days of delay.

When the airplane reached its destination and landed, everyone prepared to get off the plane. It was then that all the torture of the long delay and the last year of being apart quickly evaporated from his mind as he stepped out of the door and onto the steps that took him to his wife and daughter.

Words could not express the joy he felt as he saw Bonnie with Victoria in her arms. He didn't walk, but rather sped down the steps, straight to his wife and daughter. He could feel his body trembling with excitement as he ran and embraced them both. He hadn't felt this nervous, and so full of joy, since his wedding day.

Victoria just watched as this man hugged her mother. Her head perched back and her eyes opened wide as though she were unable to grasp the transaction taking place between the two grown-ups.

Mike and Bonnie cried tears of joy to be in each other's arms again. He eyed his little girl for the first time. She was already ten months old, not a little infant like in all the snapshots. Would she allow this strange man to hold her?

Bonnie had pointed him out every day in a portrait, explaining that the person in the photograph was her daddy. The little girl's eyes wandered, studying him from head to toe, then back to his face, as he cracked a smile with tears misting in his eyes.

"Dada," her tiny voice sounded as she smiled and her arms reached to him. That's all Mike needed to make his homecoming the best he had ever dreamed. He reached for his baby girl and squeezed her with all his might. All the memories of death and blood vanished from his mind while he held the bundle of life in his arms.

For Mike, his journey of life had taken the best turns that he ever imagined. The ride home was filled with thoughts of happy moments of the past and brightest ones for the future as he held his little girl who never removed her eyes from him. She insisted on sitting in her daddy's lap, learning everything she could about the man who had helped to bring her into this world. The one man who would protect her and her mother from any peril that life presensted.

As he watched her continue to eye him while she stroked his face, he couldn't help but wonder just what she was thinking.

The beginning of life was indeed a mystery. He imagined her life would have just as many developments in it, as he had conquered and endured in his. As he considered his age, he knew he was well into the halfway mark of man's life span, whereas his little angel's was just beginning.

He sighed, as his mind would not cease its wanderings of all his journeys from his birth to becoming a man. He had not been presented a silver spoon when he entered this world, nor a document saying he would have everything easy and to his advantage. There had been no promises signifying no tears, or sorrows, or pain. No words written in blood or ink stating all was fair in the world that everyone entered at birth. Happiness had to be worked at. It just didn't happen.

The same way with love and earning money to support a family. Nothing was free in this world, always it had to be planted and worked to get it to grow.

He smiled again as he watched the young child. Those were the precious things in life that didn't cost a dime. A warm hug, a loving smile, a kind word. Yes, those were precious jewels beyond compare. Things that his dear mother had bestowed on all her children in the few years she had spent on this earth with her family. The same things that he so wanted to give his child or other children in his lifetime.

As he thought of his own days growing up in a family with little money, he knew what years he had spent with his family had been years filled with much love. A love that only his dear mother had been able to show toward all her beloved children.

A boy's journey from birth to man indeed consisted of travels and obstacles that only he could tell, live, and share. Looking into his own child's eyes, there were more journeys for him, more years of happiness and caring to share with anyone he encountered along the way. He would see that always there would be a kind word bestowed on any far and near.

Today as he witnessed the beauty of his homeland once again, and smelled the sweetness of freedom, he knew his journey was still ongoing, with more fun adventures to share.

Oh, yes, he thought to himself, the journey he had been on was different by far, but it was absolutely magnificent to be back home, with a family he loved so dear. If anything, the dreadful jungle he had only left a few days past had this time turned him from a boy into a man.

A Burning Fire Out Of Control
The Family Portrait

The war was over for some, but for others the sound of the battle continued to rage on. Not only in the hearts and minds of the men who were still there, or those who had been in the midst of the fighting, but it had extended into the homes of families whose husbands had been to the catastrophic setting whose toll claimed far too many lives. The All-American war had broken out in the homes of thousands of military families as husbands and wives had to adjust to the closeness again. Before, each was on his own. But with the soldier's return, everything had to revert back to what it was before the war created a separation.

But now after the soldiers returned from the war to their wives back home, some marriages ended in trial separations, others in a final divorce. The ones who had to cope with the stress of it all were the children. If only parents could be in the children's shoes for a moment to hear the cries or pleadings from the soft voices of the young. These children hadn't asked to be born into the world, so why did they have to contend with the agony from parents? That was when life was not fair or kind to the little children. It was during this time their feelings were edged out, forgotten. Yet they would have to learn to live with the new development.

Bonnie had witnessed the change in her husband over the months. What had started out like a second honeymoon, upon his arrival from the war, only lasted for a few short months. After being transferred to Louisiana, things began to shift drastically for the young married couple. One thing that didn't change was the love he had for his young daughter. That was one thing no one could take away from him. He and Bonnie may have had arguments, but Victoria would never be affected by any of their quarrels.

In his own mind, he still carried feelings of love for Bonnie, but the war left wounds on him that needed to be healed. The hours of being a sergeant at the new fort were taking him away from Bonnie. Afterwards, he joined some of the other men for drinks, but one led into many for the aging instructor. It never affected his job, but his marriage seemed to be headed for the rocks.

He almost hated to go home to her. Every time he had had one too many, she was always the understanding, loving wife, welcoming him with open, inviting arms. It was enough to make him want to throw up. Didn't she ever get mad, or want to walk out on him? Had the war left her with any scars from their year of separation?

No longer did he feel like the brave, strong man who had left home to protect the rights of others. Instead he felt remorse, hate—almost like a child again. The bottle was drowning his sorrow, his troubles.

Thinking back to the days of hiding in the fox holes, dodging all the many bullets, he shed no tears this time. But once before in that jungle when he suspected immediate death, he had cried. Now there would be no more tears for this man, or so he thought.

His little daughter, Victoria, always waited for her daddy to enter the door at night. She never smelled his alcohol or felt the pain in his heart. All she saw was the man who came home every night and gave her a hug and kiss good night.

At times Bonnie resented the time father and daughter shared. In a way she was bitter toward Mike, but she knew his past had been so unhappy, she didn't want him to hurt anymore. Her love for him was enough to carry them through all the rough times ahead.

Their love life had dwindled to practically nothing, so that it came almost a surprise to discover she was pregnant with another child. Surely this would change him back to the sweet, tender man she had fallen in love with.

There had been times he had sought to run to another woman's arms to see if Bonnie would leave him for good. He had only thought of the affair, never once did he permit himself to sleep with another woman. That was one taboo he never wanted to break—*at this time*.

He wasn't good for Bonnie any more. Didn't she see that? After years of growing older, he decided his life was not supposed to be happy, but miserable. With each passing day he would drill this into his mind, hoping soon he would come to terms with it.

After the second child was born, another girl, Mike and Bonnie took a two-week vacation. She insisted they visit her grandparents, on her mother's side. They lived on a farm and the quietness of the area would be good for all of them. The atmosphere had indeed been blissful. Mike was able to clear his head and set things in their proper order. The grandparents demonstrated to him a family love he never knew ex-

isted. Their large family of five boys and three girls reminded
him of another family that would have shared such love if
tragedy had not struck. He thought of his past actions, with
the war and the bottle. For a time he had shut Bonnie out,
hating her very touch. He was so afraid of losing something so
important to him.

The day before their vacation drew to a close, she confessed to her husband that she loved him so much that if a divorce was what he wanted, she would let him go to do what
he chose.

It had been hard for her to have to endure such agony the
past year with his bout with the bottle, but she had stood by
his side because he had filled an empty void in her life. This,
he found odd coming from a family that shared love by the
pound. Her words astonished him.

"You think just because a portrait presents a pretty picture that all is right with the world, Mike. Well I have news
for you...it isn't. My parents have had a good deal of fights,
short spats, separations, and trying times, Throughout it all
they pulled together as a family, working to make it right, not
only for the sake of their children but for themselves as well."

She sighed, then continued.

"As for me, it sure hasn't been easy living with two
brothers who are a constant harassment, and a retired Master
Sergeant for a father, who spoke to his children as if in the
military. He loved us more than anything in this world, but
his military background was part of our way of life. We ate,
slept and breathed military."

She paused to take a deep breath.

"For me, that wasn't fun. My life was sheltered, separated from friends and family. When it was time to pick up

and move to another location, we had to go where the Army said to go. I developed loneliness, a certain void of knowing no one. Always wondering, was I destined to stay in my own parent's home for an eternity?

"When I first met you, and we started dating, there was a special trait about you that I had never found in another human being. I can't really point out what it was exactly, but it was there, drawing me to you. Your eyes were like signals drawing me into a well of love, deeper and deeper. A lot of people kidded me, asking why would I want to marry a man who was so much older than me, who was a very stern Sergeant in the United States Army. But all I knew at the time was this was the man I wanted to share my life until death do us part. The one to have children with, to cook meals for...to share our old age with, to..."

She stopped in mid sentence, unable to finish. Tears had begun to fill her eyes. It was going to be harder than she realized to permit him to leave. She was willing to sacrifice her happiness so the children could have a father and mother, but that she wouldn't tell him. Never did she wish him to feel compelled to stay in a loveless marriage. With his distance, she had often wondered if he had even loved her any of the years of their marriage.

He reached and took hold of her hand. There was warmth with this grasp, something she hadn't felt in a long time. Her gaze roamed to his face. She saw tears flow steadily down his cheeks—something she hadn't seen from him in a good while. His words came out, chopped and choking from the tears, but what he allowed himself to say came directly from his heart.

"Bonnie, I have been so unfair to you. I was selfish, thinking only of myself. I never knew someone as lovely as you could have a void, an emptiness in her life. I want a fresh start with you, Victoria and Renée. At first I had reasoned that I needed to push you away from me, but after being here, with your grandparents, I know now I need you more than ever. If you will have me, I want to come back and make our family the one it should have been this past year. Together we can work things out for the better. I need to learn to commit and not to be afraid to trust another human being. I implore you; please don't leave me...please."

It was an earnest cry for help; they embraced, sharing tears of joy and sorrow. The barrier between the two would never be closed again. A few spats would abound as in any marriage, but the worst conflict that had overshadowed them in the past, they hoped would never be mentioned or brought up again. There would be no more clouds to darken their days as husband and wife, or force them to even consider a separation or ending of their marriage. No, not at this time. The burning fire had been quenched for good or at least that was what they thought. The journey that was ahead of them had yet to be traveled. For now, they would only think of each day and nothing more.

For Mike, he knew that his journey from a boy into a man wasn't even half over.

A Father for All the Right Reasons
The Loss

Bonnie sat sleeping in her mother's Victorian high back chair. Her father lay on the couch. Victoria and Reneé sat nearby, watching their grandfather grimace in agonizing pain. Just looking at this once strong man was almost too much for her to bear. All throughout his years never had he given up on anything, but as she watched him this time, she knew his frail, weak appearance was not a good sign.

She remembered how her body trembled every time she picked up a magazine or a newspaper and read an article about cancer, the killer of so many. In some of the stories, many had survived through treatments; other had hung on for a few months to a few years before they died.

Never when she read any of these cases did she ever imagine her own father would have the disease. This was her daddy, the man who had worked all his years to support and care for all his family. He was always busy doing, not only for his own, but also for anyone who needed help. He was always taking time out to benefit others.

Her eyes began to observe yet another image of him stretched out on the couch, warmly covered in a blanket. It hurt her in a way that she had never experienced pain. This kind, gentle, hard working man, who never slowed down and who was considered ageless, was slowly dwindling to nothing. For the past two months he had been shifted back and forth from one doctor to another as each continued to run tests after tests on him. They kept insisting they needed to pinpoint his exact problem and area of pain before any treatments could be administered.

In the meantime, they would prescribe painkillers, but still they only stopped the pain for a little while, and then he was lying, suffering once again. At times she would think of the movie where the mother sees her daughter lying in the hospital bed suffering. She then confronts the nurses, screaming that it was time for her daughter's medication. She, too, felt like screaming, if it would rid his body of the terrible pain. But the mere act would never cast it from his body.

The doctors continued to inform them they would have to know the exact problem before dispensing any form of drug. They could be sued for any type of malpractice. She fully understood the doctor's viewpoint on the situation, but still it pained her to see him in this suffering state. Her heart went out to anyone who had to watch someone dear suffering in torment with no release of pain. It was a time when others were willing to take over the pain so they no longer would have to endure it; but that, too, was always the impossible dream. So they wait, they pray, and love that person and try every way possible to make their life a little more comfortable.

She noticed it was beginning to take a heavy toll on her mother with each passing day. Her beloved mother would wait on him, almost at his beck and call, because it would hurt him to move about. She spent most of her days by his side.

Even when they would have to go into town to buy a few groceries, her thoughts continued to be with her husband. She would worry until they pulled into the driveway, if her dear husband was all right, and especially still alive.

Even though Bonnie and Mike, and Bonnie's brothers, were there for him while she was away, she constantly wondered how he was. She was not at peace with herself until she was back by his side.

Bonnie's youngest daughter, Reneé, could see the strain in her grandmother's face and she would tell her mother how sad grandmother looked. Bonnie realized this, but was unable to stop her sadness, and sorrow. In her own way, Bonnie explained to her young daughter that her grandmother had to endure her own suffering. It was something she had to deal with on her own. Each night Bonnie would pass by her daughter's room and hear a special prayer being offered for her grandparents. One, that her grandmother would be able to cope with the changes she faced, and the other, for her granddaddy to be cured, to have enough strength to endure the pain that was not going to go away.

She remembered how he used to be active every day of the week. After spending twenty-one years in the Army, he retired but needed to continue with some kind of work so he chose to go into the mobile home business. Managing the mobile homes kept him relatively busy. But regardless of how late it was or how tired he may have ached when he arrived home, he would make sure he made time for his five granddaughters. It didn't matter if it was to check the oil or antifreeze or anything in their cars, the man took sheer pleasure in catering to his beautiful granddaughters' needs.

If they needed to practice their tennis or softball techniques, he would go out in the yard and join in, as if one of the kids. Whether it was building a birdhouse, to making a simulated volcano for a school project, he never failed his granddaughters. If it was in his reach, he was always there at every turn. The granddaughters never hesitated in boasting what a *grand* granddad he was. They admired his untiring energy.

As the falling leaves began ushering in the change of seasons, October brought a change for him too. He began showing signs of illness more throughout his body. By December, the gusty, wintry winds approached with bitter coldness, as Bonnie's father seemed to age so much in such a short time span. Mike would come in from work talking about how thin and elderly her father looked. He missed the talks that the two of them had grown to share with each other.

Food began to make him sick to his stomach and he was losing sleep because of back and leg pain. With each passing day he was becoming weaker and weaker. Even getting up to take a shower or shaving was painful. He reminded Bonnie of an etching drawn on canvas, after the impediment of rain or foul weather had released its nature on its sketched surface, blotting its once beautiful features. Just as the soil had rinsed the etching, so had his pain rinsed his once rugged features.

By late December the tests began—in abundance. First there was blood work, next came the x-rays. Other tests consisted of running tubes up through him to do a biopsy to check for prostate cancer, while yet another consisted of a light running down him for a biopsy to check for cancer in the lungs— a tumor-like shape had been discovered on one of his lungs. When he was also diagnosed with prostate and advanced lung cancer, Mother was in tears.

Even with some of the tests conclusive, the doctors wanted to pinpoint why he was having a good deal of pain in his back and leg. All the tests were causing enough excruciating pain alone; why couldn't they give him something stronger for the pain—now, this instant!

The doctors did indeed prescribe stronger medications, even morphine and other drugs to control the pain he was experiencing. During this time everyone sat and waited for the outcome.

Even as Bonnie watched her once strong-willed father slowly dwindling with the pangs of death, she realized he needed to explain to her that he didn't worry so much over his imminent death. Instead, he worried if his loving wife would be cared for and have enough money when he was gone from this earth. There had been so much money already that had been spent on his medication and hospitalization. There was insurance and money set aside for any unforeseen, unexpected emergencies, but he didn't want to leave his wife a widow, with nothing to live on. With tender words, spoken in withering sorrow, he told Bonnie his closest thoughts and concerns.

She inhaled a fresh breath, as the words that issued from his lips began to melt her heart. She had an urge to cry and really scream from the top of her lungs, but she wouldn't allow her loving father who raised and cared for her all these years, to hear or see her express sorrow. Instead, she grasped his withering, wrinkled hand that was mostly bone from so much weight loss and placed a loving kiss on his forehead.

"Daddy, you haven't any need to worry about Mother. You took care of us all these years. We are going to make sure we are there for the both of you. I will never discard you or

Mother in your olden years. You nourished and cared for us from day one and even after we married and had our own children to raise. You were there caring for us when we needed you. Please don't worry about Mother. I will make sure she gets everything she needs. All I want you to do now is rest. You need to get your strength back. We've got a baseball game to finish playing."

She wanted to say more but her words were beginning to break. She allowed his hand to go back down by his side, as she wiped away a tear from her eye. One thing she never wanted him to see was the tears.

He cast her a half grin when she informed him there was a baseball game to finish. In his heart, he knew there would be no more games for his body, not ever in this life. It was when he gradually closed his eyes, finally drifting off into a restful slumber that she was able to leave his side.

She went to a far room where he couldn't see the heavy downpour of tears. As painful as the moment was to her system, it was a relief to release the sorrowful burden.

That night Bonnie lay in her bed wondering if that was the night her mother would phone telling of his death. They knew there wasn't much time left for the dear man. All the tests had been concluded. What few treatments had been administered to the frail man were now curtailed. The cancer was so widespread in his system that there was no help for him. All they had left together was the last few months they would be sharing by his side.

While Bonnie's father was lying with his own suffering, there was a quiet grief her mother was also experiencing, the underlying disease of helplessness and waiting for his demise.

Would it be during the night or day? He had been sent

home to finish out his days since there was nothing else to be done by the doctors. His state was classified and stamped— terminally ill. They might as well have said, hopeless, no more time, your guess is as good as mine.

Bonnie burned inside to even consider such a thought, but for some reason she couldn't help this feeling she had to go through. She resented that her father was being taken from her. The mere thought was eating away at her, almost like a cankerous worm! Just as her own mother was standing tall and erect for her children, she, too, had to project the same feeling for her daughters. Mike stood by her side fully understanding the true meaning of loss. No matter what age, a child truly hated to witness the death of a parent.

In her heart she spoke silently to him, words never heard, except by her subconscious mind.

Dearest Daddy of mine, I have never been able to speak well to you in person. I always liked to express myself to you with words on paper, feeling as if I could communicate with you better. I wish I could have your pain. If I could erase it all from your body, I would in an instant, but that I know won't happen. For now, I give you my deepest love and prayers. I want you to know I love you more than words could ever express. This is one daughter who will never forget your gentle kindness to us and others.

A few days later the cancer had won. He was gone from their midst. Bonnie had been able to express her thoughts to him before he passed away. She wasn't really sure if he had understood everything she had said, but in a way she was certain he had. She recalled he stretched out his hand when she walked into his room, casting her a loving smile, as if to say everything was going to be all right for everyone. Three hours later, he was gone. It was quick.

Even while Bonnie pondered her loving memories of him, especially of that last day he took hold of her hand and gave her a tender smile, that one special moment continued to cloud her mind. It wasn't there to damper dark forbidden shadows of sorrow, but rather to reflect on all the tears of joy, and sometimes pain of all the loving thoughts and sweetness he brought to her life and others. She considered him the right father for all the right reasons.

Not only had he been a good father to her, but to Mike as well. The First Sergeant had been a man that he had grown to love and for whom he held deep respect. One with whom he had shared many conversations in his later years. Close-knit times that he would miss, just as he had missed the times he had shared with his dear departed mother. It was just another trip of his journey that he held close to his heart. Yes indeed, he too, considered the First Sergeant the right father for all the right reasons.

The Calm before the Storm
The Unexpected Turn

After all the trials and things that he had endured, Mike never imagined that he would have the terrible midlife crisis that hit him. He had lost his mother at the tender age of ten. He had been separated from his siblings. Even after all the years behind him, there had been no knowledge of baby sister's whereabouts. Would he ever be able to see her before their life ended upon this earth? He had met and married a wonderful woman who had given him three beautiful children. Still, as he grew another year older, he was feeling emptiness. With the passing of his dear father-in-law there had been really no one to talk to. He had missed their evening conversations where they'd used military jargon.

His baby girl had just turned eight-months-old, and the other two children were five and seven. Why was he considering ending something that was so beautiful? He hadn't meant for Bonnie to hear the phone conversation. She just happened to pick up the phone by mistake.

"Yes. It will be okay. I can meet you after the play. Don't worry about anything. Yes, I love you, too."

Bonnie had kept it to herself for over a month. Their marriage had grown distant. She had gone through a similar feeling before in their marriage, but this time it was stronger. His long days at work, then going to night school were not only playing havoc on their marriage, but on his life as well. It was just before Christmas when everything hit the fan.

"Bonnie, could we go into the dining room and talk? I need to show you something."

They left the children admiring the decorative Christmas tree. After they sat down at the table, Mike pulled out a small box.

"This is for you."

"Honey, Christmas is only six days away. I can wait."

"I would like for you to open it now...please," he urged.

Bonnie opened the tiny jewelry box. Inside was a gold necklace with a tiny gold-like box attached to the end of it with a small shaped diamond on the corner. It had the initials MRF.

"These are your initials, Mike."

"I thought that you might like it."

"It is very lovely."

"Now for the bad news."

Bonnie was taken aback.

"Tomorrow the sheriff will be delivering divorce papers here. I guess you've noticed how distant we have grown. I don't know what is wrong with me. I'm just not happy anymore. It isn't you. It isn't the children."

"So just like that, you are going to toss what years we have together out the window? I suppose the person I caught you talking to on the phone a number of times is behind this?"

"We are just friends. We spend a lot of time studying. I'm sorry. I know that I am hurting you."

"Hurting me? You give me a necklace with your initials on it. You tell me you are filing for divorce. We have three small children. It is six days until Christmas. How noble of you to stress that you are hurting me. Very honorable of you, Mike."

"I didn't want this confrontation. I thought about not saying a word and just allowing the sheriff to show up with the papers."

"How selfish!"

"Look, I want this to be a nice parting. I didn't mean to hurt you. I'm going to make sure the children are taken care of."

"You bet your life you are. I wish that my dad were here to see this. He would be so disappointed in you, Mike. Look at our children. How are they going to be without a father?"

"They aren't losing a father. I will always be their father."

"Sure, but with a different home. Are you moving in with this person?"

"I don't know what I am going to do now. I am going through a rough time. Why can't you understand?"

"These children need a father."

"Bonnie, listen to me. *I am still going to be their father.*"

"Just not here. Guess you and your ole friend will have some fun time together being childless. What is it Mike? Your life was so miserable growing up without both parents that you want to inflict that same sorrow on your children? Why would you want to do that to them?"

"I'm leaving. I can't get you to listen to anything I'm saying."

"You are filing for divorce and wonder why I'm not listening? Okay, what about Christmas? What about the girls?" Bonnie was trembling.

Baby Michelle crawled into the dining room. "Da, da."

Mike picked her up, hugged her tightly then gave her a

kiss. "I love you, baby girl."

"Mike, can't we work something out? Perhaps separate bedrooms? Anything?"

Mike carried Michelle back into the living room. "Daddy has to go away for a few days, girls. Listen to your mother." He sat Michelle by Victoria and Reneé.

"What about Christmas?" little Reneé asked, her pretty blue eyes opened wide.

Mike broke into tears.

"Are you happy now? See what you are doing to your family? No good can come from any of this." Bonnie sobbed.

"I'll keep in touch."

"Don't bother. The girls and I don't need you. We will be fine. Just go about your business and by all means, don't worry about your family!" Tears were pouring down Bonnie's face.

Mike walked to the door and put on his coat. Bonnie lost control. She ran and grabbed hold of his leg.

"Mike, please! Don't leave me. Don't leave us. I love you."

He pulled her arms away. "Don't do this. I said I'll keep in touch."

"If you go out that door, don't you ever come back. You'll never see these children again—ever!"

Mike took his small bag and eyed the girls one last time. He wiped the tears from his eyes then closed the door behind him. Bonnie sat on the floor grief stricken. The tears were heavy, the wailing loud. The girls came to her side.

"It's okay, Mommy," Victoria said. "Daddy is only going on a trip.

Bonnie eyed her three beautiful daughters. She wrapped them in her arms. Mike didn't realize what he was giving up.

The sheriff did arrive by noon with the papers. He told her

it was equally hard on him because Mike and Bonnie were like family.

Mike phoned and asked could he spend Christmas Eve with the girls. He would sleep on the couch and leave that morning. Bonnie said he might as well stay for Christmas dinner. He accepted.

It was a joyous feeling, watching the girls open the gifts. They were allowed to open one Christmas Eve, then the rest the next morning when Santa arrived. The girls didn't mind. They knew Santa had many stops. Mike had a fun time with the family. Bonnie hoped that he would get out of this stage. After all, he had stopped drinking after getting out of the military. Why couldn't he free himself from this, too?

She recalled how his drinking days had almost destroyed the family. There had been times she had poured the alcohol all down the drain. Once, she had even put a few drops of lighter fluid in it hoping he would stop. Twice he had pushed her, and held a knife to her throat. He always said she was lying. He never remembered how he behaved in his drunken stupor. She was seven months pregnant at the time with Michelle. Victoria and Reneé had been very young but they witnessed it. She remembered they took off running to their bedroom and closed the door.

After the alcohol made him sleepy, Bonnie would go in and talk to the girls. "Daddy was only playing. He would never hurt Mommy." She would tell them this over and over. It was something their young minds would never forget—even when they grew older. It was after the birth of Michelle that Mike decided to go cold turkey with the booze. He hadn't touched it since. She remembered someone handing him a beer at a party. He opened it then turned it upside down until the can was empty.

He said he would never touch another drop again. He had rid himself of that demon, why not this one, too?

"Bonnie, I told the girls bye. I'm leaving now."

Tears filled her eyes.

"I don't want another scene, Bonnie."

"So noble of you, Mike. Once again, poor Mike gets what he wants."

He put on his jacket.

"I've seen a lawyer," Bonnie admitted.

"I don't want a contested divorce."

"This is two ways. You opened the door when you had the sheriff serve me with the divorce papers. He said I can get you good for child support."

"Don't threaten me. Those are my children. I will provide for them."

"Really? You drained out our checking and savings account, closing them behind my back. On top of that, you took the money out that my dad had given the children before he died. What kind of human steals from his children? You are one sick human, Michael! You need help. I'm going to make sure you never see your children again. I bet you sleep well at night, with your little friend, knowing you are practically sending us to welfare."

Mike eyed the girls playing with their toys. "I'll call."

"Like I said, don't bother. We really don't need you. And if I want to contest this divorce, Mister, I will." Bonnie shot him a stern look just before he walked out the door.

A couple of days before New Year's, Bonnie decided to do a role reversal. She went to Mike's office.

"Hi. Can we talk?"

"It depends," he said, closing a file. "Is it going to be civil?"

"Yes. I'm tired of fighting."

"Are the children okay?"

"The children are great. I left them with Mom. We are going to rent a movie tonight and have our popcorn and M&M night. You know how the girls love that."

He nodded.

"Mike, I've been doing some thinking. You can use the portable TV if you need to take it."

"Oh, really?"

"Yes. In fact you can come by the house this afternoon and get what items you might need in your new home."

"What's the catch?"

"We have three beautiful children. We have to think about them and what role all this may be playing on them. We need to be friends, not enemies."

"Your attitude certainly has changed."

"I'm doing this for the children. They are the innocent ones here. Once we are divorced, I can go on with my life, too. There are other fish in the sea."

He eyed her strangely.

"Oh, I'm sorry. Was I supposed to sit around by myself and just take care of the girls? You have a life. I have one, too. I'm not a bad looking woman, Mike. I'm sure there is a man out there who would be a loving husband to me and great father to the children. So you're welcome to come by this afternoon."

"I might do that."

"Would you like to come over for dinner New Year's Day? I was thinking of preparing duck. I know how you like it. That is, if you have no plans. I can always change the menu, too."

"You hate duck."

"But you like it. It's New Year's. You know, out with the

old, in with the new."

"The menu is fine. What time?"

"Around noon?"

"I'll be there. Give me an hour to finish here and I'll come by and get those things."

"Sure, I'll see you then."

Bonnie fought back the tears all the way to the car. She wouldn't allow him to see her pain. He had wanted to leave once before but had changed his mind. She was hoping he would eventually change his mind this time, too.

New Year's Eve proved to be fruitful for Bonnie. Her strategic plan had worked. Mike had phoned. He didn't want the lifestyle he had. He missed his children. He missed Bonnie.

"I know you don't believe me, but I am sorry. I do miss you, Bonnie. I love you."

Bonnie's heart jumped for joy. She wouldn't tell Mike. He would be back that night. They would be husband and wife again.

Bonnie put the girls to bed. After taking a bubble bath, she dressed in a black gown she had purchased for Christmas. Tonight she and Mike would be together again. She would have the man she had fallen head over heels in love with, not only in her heart, but her life as well.

Just before midnight there was still no sign of Mike. Bonnie figured he had changed his mind. She was about to turn off the lights when the phone rang.

"Bonnie, I am still coming home. Please believe me. There's just one problem. My friend isn't taking this well. She's talking about jumping off a bridge."

Oh, really? Bonnie thought. *Maybe I should come give her a push.*

"Bonnie, are you there?"

"So what are you saying, Mike?"

"I am coming home. It may not be tonight, but tomorrow for sure. Please believe me. Most importantly—please trust me."

"I do, Mike," she lied. "The girls and I will be here."

"I love you, Bonnie," he said before hanging up.

Bonnie eyed herself in the mirror. "You stupid idiot. You get all goo-goo for this guy again who breaks your heart but has to be there for her. Look at you. Just take him back like nothing has happened!"

She took the gown off and packed it away. She would never wear it for him. Trust him, ha. She had been through a horrific ordeal. That would never happen. For the next fifteen years she would end up always doubting his every word. She would never allow him to see it. Mike would sense it, she was sure of that. He would have to move heaven and earth to win her trust again. He was in for a fight for his life. All Bonnie saw anymore was a business arrangement for the sake of the children.

In time, Mike too, realized that this journey that he had stamped on his heart was something he would never be able to reverse. It was yet another journey in his life from a boy into a man.

Firstborn
The Bonding of a Family

Mike watched the little face with the soft milk-colored skin follow his movements as he got out of the car and walked over toward her. She was so beautiful. Every time he arrived home from a hard day at the office she would be at the front door waiting for him to come in, give her a little tickle on the stomach, and throw her up in the air.

He hadn't been there for her arrival. She was close to eleven-months-old before he actually got to see his firstborn. Since then he had always been there for her. Mike loved his firstborn. Perhaps it was the fact that she would be the first to leave. Then again that didn't always work in some cases, but there was something always about the firstborn.

He would often rewind all those moments, in his mind, as she grew into an adorable, beautiful young girl. From the terrible two's to her teenage years, Victoria had been a handful. Even with her sisters, Reneé and Michelle, Victoria's actions seemed to stand out more. And as he eyed himself every morning in the mirror, he indeed had the gray hair to prove his worries. Just another process of his path along life's journey, he told himself.

There had been temper-tantrums, the constant asking of

questions, especially when it came to why, why, why. The young child was curious, wishing to know everything that was going on around her. Mike would check his hair every morning not only to see if another new gray strand was visible but also to see if he were gradually going bald as well.

With every question or fit she threw, there was another dimension to her that tugged at your heart, allowing you to forget all her quirky behavior. He often wondered if this was how it was when he was growing up with his mother and father. It had been such a long time since he had been small that he couldn't remember ever being so inquisitive with his parents. Especially not with his father.

When it came to his firstborn, there had been the glowing face that looked up at you, grabbing hold of your pants leg after you walked in from a hard day's work. Then the funny face she presented when she tried a new vegetable, or the expression on her face just before she'd fall headfirst into a plate of spaghetti because she was so tired, yet was fighting sleep. That had been a moment he wished he had captured on video.

When she excitedly watched a cartoon or kiddy movie, her little hands would clap with delight. With every ounce of strength her young body could carry, she would stay wide-eyed until the last yawn faded into sleep.

And if she happened to be watching the movie with the flying car or the flying woman with the umbrella, one knew never to shut off the television for those two movies. That alone would open her tired eyes immediately.

After she finally surrendered to the tiredness, Mike would cuddle her in his arms, and then carry her to bed. "Good night, Daddy," were always her words as her head hit the pillow. He would always give her a kiss on the forehead before turning off her night-light.

With each birthday they would recall the year before, exploring all the events that had transpired. The years of old age were quickly approaching. He longed to enjoy every moment. He never knew if it was because she was the firstborn, or because with her, he, too, had been learning the stages of parenting, whereas with Reneé and Michelle, it had come more readily for him and Bonnie. There was just a force that threw him closer to her.

Mike knew she would be the first to enter school, the first to graduate, and most likely the first that would marry and leave home. Always the first held a special part in your heart, as well as the last. The middle child and those in between had certain traits, all harboring characteristics that parents could only sense and hold dear. He did recall a few moments of those in his childhood when he was born and the children that arrived afterward.

The times he had shared with his firstborn stayed lodged in the back of his mind. There had been a good many great ones that made up for the worse times. When he first witnessed her in her cap and gown walking on stage to retrieve her diploma, there was such an intense emotional impact that he felt he would burst if he didn't run up to the stage with her. For twelve years she had absorbed her education. He was so proud of her that graduation day as she stood in cap and gown. The feeling was inexpressible by mere words.

As he watched her from afar he thought of her first date. The thought of allowing his angel to go out with a male species had been almost too much to bear. But he took it in stride, especially after Bonnie reminded him of their first date. After careful reasoning, and having a hard talk with the boy, he allowed the date to take place. He imagined most fathers were the same the first time the daughter wanted to go out.

He never let Victoria know, but all the times her mother was waiting up for the couple to return home, he, too, was lying in bed, waiting to hear the car drive up, and his little angel come through the door. It was only after her arrival that he was able to rest the remainder of the night. Luckily for him, the dates weren't too frequent, or he would have never gotten any sleep.

With the passing of the years, even with his long work hours, and Bonnie's as well, money for college tuition was short. This had hurt him a good deal. All his life he had planed how he wanted his children to have a good college education. They would need that in the job world. No one told him that college tuition would skyrocket with the years. Victoria was the first to hear the conversation.

"Bonnie, I don't know what to do. We're just making it now. I want them to attend college. This is important to me. I want them to have the things in life that I was never able to have growing up."

"Mike, the girls know that you have done plenty for them—for us. You don't need to be worrying yourself over this. Stress isn't good."

"Mother's right," Victoria interrupted. Reneé and Michelle were by her side. "Daddy, I want to help. If it means having to get a part-time job, I want to do my share. You don't need to be knocking yourself out over this."

Reneé was the second to speak. "I second the motion. I can help, too. You never wanted us to work while in school, but most of my friends do that. As for my grades, they will stay high. I won't let any of my schoolwork fall behind. I just need you to sign a work release form giving your permission."

Mike felt a tear coming. "I don't know what to say. I wanted to be the sole breadwinner. I didn't even want your mother outside the home working. When Michelle got older, she wanted to spread her wings and help."

"It was a good choice, Daddy," Michelle mentioned. "Just look at all the nice stuff I got from Mom working." She laughed her funny laugh.

"Silly girl, come here, and give your ole dad a hug."

"Can I have a car?"

"Michelle, you're too young for a car."

She sported a silly grin.

"If you sign this work release form, I can apply for work at this barbecue restaurant," Reneé said, handing him the form.

"Guess you were hoping that I would say yes, perhaps, young lady?" Mike said, raising his eyebrow.

"There's another restaurant hiring, too," Victoria said. "I'm going to apply tomorrow. It will help some."

"What positions are open?" Mike questioned.

"They're both for waitresses," Reneé answered.

"That is very hard work, girls. Some of the customers can get nasty. I've seen the way they treat some of these young girls."

"We know, Daddy. It's only temporary until something else comes along. This is what Reneé and I want to do. We just need your permission. Our family has stuck together through the good and the bad. Nothing should separate us now. Our family helps one another. Right, Mom?" Victoria looked at Bonnie and smiled.

Bonnie remembered the year Mike wanted the divorce. She had lived in a loveless marriage for a long time after that. She would tell him they had a business relationship more than a marriage. The more she thought of that, the more she would look at the children. She knew she had made the right choice. It had been tough hanging in there, trusting someone again, but watching the girls grow up into beautiful, disciplined young women told Bonnie she had certainly made the right choice.

"Mike, let them have a chance. I have all the faith in everything they do."

"Daddy, my girlfriend's podiatrist told her that his wife worked four years as a waitress and with all the tips she made, she was able to help pay her way through college. We will make sure to tell them what shifts we can work. There are a lot of places eager to help a student on the work/study program," Reneé commented.

"And I'll be sure to stress I really need the day shift. But I can't always promise they'll give me that one," Victoria said.

"Guess that leaves little ole me," Michelle said. "I will help more around the house."

"Yeah, right." Reneé laughed.

They eyed each other and cracked a smile. They knew Michelle hated any form of housework.

Reneé and Victoria each turned in an application and were hired the same day. From day one, the job was very tiring, especially on the feet. This was an on the go, all the time, type of job. Reneé went in right after school. Victoria was allowed to work during the daytime. She had also put in applications for secretarial positions if they happened to have an opening.

One day Mike surprised Victoria and dropped in for lunch. He watched as her slim body scurried to take the orders then bring them out. At one point he had thought she would turn out to be the slow poke of the brood but not anymore. She was always on the go, especially now.

When he sat down at the booth, he asked to have her for his waitress. A glow spread through him when she waited on him, as well as others. It made him feel good to see his daughter pleasing the customers with her speediness and warm smile. When he started to leave, he left her a generous tip, not because she was his daughter, but because of the way she had handled herself distributing everything to his satisfaction.

He observed all the other waitresses also on call. It was a shame that some who came in to eat didn't bother leaving a tip, and those who did only left a few pennies. He shook his head. If it weren't for these waitresses, just how would they get their meal brought to their table? Mike wanted to scream. He knew the girls were only making peanuts an hour, yet people didn't bother leaving them a dime for their service. There were a few that left tips, but others just brushed it aside. Of course, he had family that was the same way. Some people just didn't understand. Even before his daughters started waitressing, he always compensated anyone's duties.

Two months later, Victoria had to change her hours. They needed her to work a few times during the night shift. It was a good drive to the restaurant from their home, so Mike agreed to drive her. He didn't want her driving alone at night.

One of the nights, after church services, Mike treated his family to dinner. Victoria had been unable to attend because of work. The restaurant was bustling with crowds of people. All the waitresses were racing as if in a marathon. It was a wonder there wasn't a collision. They had been placed in Victoria's section. She hurriedly took their order smiling the whole time. Still, Mike could see the strain of tiredness in his daughter's face. This was one job, though, that she didn't wish to give up. For the moment nothing else had become available.

Their drinks were brought out and she told them to visit the salad bar while they waited on the food. It would take a while due to the abundance of Sunday worshippers getting out of church and coming in for dinner. No sooner had they sat back down at the table, they began losing their appetite.

Across from them, three couples had been escorted to a table. The tall bald headed man kept looking around for a waitress. Mike could hear him speak but the others didn't say too much, if they did it was inaudible.

"This place is busy tonight. It may take a while before we get a waitress. Just keep your fingers crossed that it isn't that skinny one. She is so slow," the bald man remarked.

"Honey, they are probably tired and burdened with so many that it just looks like they are slow," his wife said. At least Mike figured it was his wife.

The bald headed man turned to speak to the other couples. At times his words were audible then he would lower his voice to a mumble. This continued for a few minutes. Mike had a feeling he was striking out against one of the waitresses. It was Bonnie who really heard it and kicked Mike in the leg.

"Mike, he's referring to *our* Victoria. She is the only one here by that name."

"I heard him mention her name, too, Daddy," Reneé added.

"Me, too," Michelle remarked, "and I'm ready to kick

butt."

Mike played with his salad as his ear stretched more into the conversation.

"Yeah if you eat here, you sure don't want to get that girl they call Victoria. She can never do anything right."

About that time, Victoria came bringing out the meal.

"Now, if you need anything else please let me know," she said with a smile before walking off.

Mike observed the bald headed man point her out as she walked off, telling the others that was the skinny one he had been referring to. That was all he needed to hear. Once some-one had stepped on his family, especially his daughters, that was the last straw.

"Excuse me, sir," Mike began, "did I hear you speak of Victoria, the waitress here?"

"Yes, don't get her for a waitress. She is too slow and a sorry waitress at that."

"Okay, Daddy." Michelle spoke loudly. "Can I kick his butt now?"

"Michelle, please hush," Bonnie said.

"Sir, that is my daughter you are talking about."

Mike noticed the man's wife give him a cold stare.

"Well, I wasn't aware of that. She may be a good person and all, but I have seen better waitresses in my day."

"I think she is going as fast as humanly possible. I'm not just saying that because she is my daughter. All of the wait-resses are pulling their weight double time today to get every-one's order out. I don't appreciate you sitting there and belit-tling her that way. You shouldn't call someone sorry when you don't even know them. If you think you could do better, perhaps you should apply for the job."

Michelle did a thumbs up, you go Dad.

"Well, like I said, I don't know her personally but I really don't care much for her as a waitress."

The man's wife gave him another stare. "I told you your mouth was going to start something one day. You need to learn not to be so rude."

The other two couples sat and listened. Mike got the feeling they were annoyed by the man's behavior. He seemed like the type who sought to find fault in others.

"I bet he wouldn't like it if someone complained about his shiny bald head," Reneé said, putting in her two cents.

Bonnie cast her a curt little stare.

No one really wanted to eat after that little episode. When the manager walked around checking to see if everything was all right, Mike told him the meal was fine. He mentioned everything that had been said. He even asked—would he make sure Victoria never waited on that man's table if he showed up again? He never wanted Victoria to know that he had mentioned the last part to the manager.

The manager mentioned that the gentleman was a regular who complained about everything. But he couldn't just throw him out.

Mike couldn't believe how obnoxious some people could be. It was ironic how they could always pinpoint a flaw in another human, but never see one in themselves. It wasn't long before the girls were able to switch jobs. They never forgot their days of being a waitress. Neither did Mike and Bonnie. It was a time when he had truly discovered how close-knit they were as a family. It was a journey with a family that he would always replay many times in his mind.

Sometimes You Can't Take the Boy Out of the Man
The Getaway

There comes a time in a person's life that you have to just say, "Hey, today I need a break, a get-away." So you gather your family, pack some bags and climb in the car and head for sights you've never seen.

So it was in the case of Mike and his family. After hearing so much about the fabulous sights of Stone Mountain, he knew it was time to go there. There were things pressing at work, but he knew if he didn't take the time to have some days of blissful rest, he would never get the opportunity again.

He put in for a three-day weekend holiday, then loaded the car with the wife and children and headed for Stone Mountain, Georgia.

He had been shown many a brochure on the events that he could take part in. Not to mention all the sights to snap pictures of, and even witness the Laser Show. Especially see the Laser Show, he was told. If you do nothing else, be sure to stay for it.

Since the reservations were at the Stone Mountain Inn, he was determined to do just that. His daughters didn't care what they saw. They were anxious, waiting to board the Sky Lift and go to the top of the mountain. More than anything they prayed for no rain, at least until after they had been atop the grand mountain.

The three-day excursion would have two nights spent at the famous Inn they had heard so much about. Again, the girls were looking forward to that event. They had never been able to stay overnight in a hotel before.

Just before nearing the main gate to enter the Stone Mountain Camp, they could see a view of the huge mountain area from the highway. Mike's eyes lit up like sapphires when he observed the mountain for the first time.

"Can you believe it? We're here. The mountain is only minutes ahead," he said, beaming with excitement.

Bonnie noticed his enthusiasm. Never had she seen anyone so overjoyed to see such a sight since she watched Chevy Chase in *Vacation,* when he desperately wanted to enter Wally World. Today she was getting that same show as she watched her husband's excitement. Today he was a young schoolboy again, receiving that new toy he had always wanted.

Her heart leaped as he experienced first hand such a magnificent sensation. She, too, was feeling a little giddy, but for the moment it would stay inside her heart. This was his moment and she didn't wish to spoil it. She often wondered what all he had missed growing up without the family she'd been so fortunate to have.

"There it is, girls," he stated, after paying for the ticket to get in the gate. "Our ticket to the best time we have had in a long while."

They would be unable to check into their room until three. So for the two and a half hour wait, they went to the ticket office and purchased the *Big Ticket Package,* to view at least six different events while they were at the mountain. There would be a few sights to observe before checking into the Inn. The first choice was the train that took them around the mountain. *Yes, yes, yes,* the girls chanted in unison.

Halfway around the mountain, the train slowed down, allowing those who wished to get off at Confederate Hall or the wildlife trails for the animals, to disembark and view the other sights. Another train would be back around later to pick them up.

Mike looked at his family. "What say we get off at the wildlife trails? We have a while still to wait for our room."

They all agreed.

Seeing all of the animals was a pleasure in itself. But the long distance walk, trudging up and down the winding pathway was very tiring to Bonnie and Victoria. But nevertheless, they made it an enjoyable outing. Of course heading back across the bridge, their tired legs slowed them down so they missed the first train.

"Don't worry," Mike said as he gathered a breath. "Another one will be by shortly. We'll go to the benches at the depot area and rest a spell."

"We would have made it Dad, if Mom and Victoria hadn't been such slow pokes," Michelle commented.

"Well, we'll let them have this one."

She looked at her Dad and gave him a smile. She grasped hold of his hand, while they walked across the bridge to the depot. Reneé took hold of his other hand.

The next stop was registering at their room and unloading the car. Upon entering the spacious room, they were speechless. Never had they seen such a big, roomy area. There were two huge beds, plus a long Victorian type sofa to sit on for watching television. The adjoining room had the same décor.

"Honey, have you seen the bathroom? It's huge," Bonnie

stated.

Mike listened to all of them talk nonstop as he walked over to the sofa, sat down and turned on the television for a few minutes.

"Daddy, we don't have time for TV. We've got places to go see," Reneé reminded.

"I was thinking about getting a little food before we started walking all over the place. How about it?"

"Sounds good to me," Bonnie answered. "What about eating here at the Inn? We can always choose the other places tomorrow."

The others agreed as they turned off the TV and helped Mike off the sofa.

Going into the Inn, they climbed the stairs to the second floor and were escorted to a table by a friendly young waitress. Mary was her name, but she spelled it, *Meri*. Her perky smile and sweet disposition was a most welcome sight. She was petite with short, brown hair. She would be one young girl who would remain always in their hearts once they left the mountain area.

A young girl with such a warm personality as hers, one just doesn't forget, Victoria had said. Michelle insisted the young waitress be left a sizeable tip. Bonnie and Mike agreed there would be.

After ordering their buffet lunch and finishing their meal, they told Meri goodbye and headed for the antebellum Plantation. Inside the structure that was set apart for viewing of the homes, they each found the area fascinating. With each step they took, and every word that was spoken by their tour guide after they entered the homes, everything was breathtaking. They imagined going back in time and experiencing living in such a manor. The events were truly beyond any expression of words.

Nearing the barn area, they spotted a young woman weaving rugs. Mike had to buy one. As for Bonnie, she chose a handmade footstool and allowed the man to engrave Mike's name on the top.

When they left the barnyard area, they saw another little stand was set up. An elderly husband and wife were selling some of the goods she had sewn and stitched. Michelle opted for one of her hand-sewn dolls. They were such beautiful works of art.

Victoria had other types of souvenirs on her mind. After visiting almost every gift shop that the area housed, she insisted on getting nearly every different T-shirt she saw. Each one had a different picture on its front.

With the antebellum Homes Tour concluded, a trip was made into the little country store which carried all kind of jellies, preserves and candies, galore. Naturally, Mike had to purchase many of the jars. As for Bonnie, she wanted only little cards, and books telling of the different areas of the mountain, and of the sights and their construction.

The next stop was the riverboat, *The Scarlett O'Hara.*

The girls, along with their daddy, wanted to go atop the boat. Bonnie wasn't too keen on heights, but she did join them, sitting on one of the chairs that was provided. She had no desire to look over the rail to the deep waters below.

Afterwards, the girls dashed over to try out the paddleboats. Mike got excited just watching his lovely daughters paddling away on the small yellow carriers. Yes, this was one trip he was enjoying more than anything. He wondered, if his mother had lived longer, would his parents have ever taken them on such a trip? With the lack of money and the hard times, he doubted any of that would have been possible in his home life. Things had changed with the passing of time, and the development of new jobs. He was glad that he never had to be a coal miner like his dad.

The best part came after dinner. Walking toward the mountain, they stopped and sat on the carved out rock that was similar to a picnic area, facing the front of Memorial Lawn and the mountain carving. Above their ears, atop a tree, a speaker was situated. The music was already blaring a Diet Coke commercial, as the Lasers bounced off the carving on the mountain. The light and sound extravaganza was by far the best event of the trip. It started out with different fast tunes by James Brown, and Whitney Houston, with their simulated etchings drawn out by lasers on the mountain. Then fireworks were set off and displayed in a wonderful color.

There were *oohs,* and *ahs,* as everyone felt their heart leap at such a spectacular occurrence. The song "I Wish I was in Dixie" came on, as the three men dressed to look like Jefferson Davis, Robert E. Lee, and Thomas Stonewall Jackson mounted their horses. With swords, they galloped off to fight the war. It was followed by Elvis's version of "Glory, Glory," as the tired, worn, General Lee passed by on his horse, observing all the graves that already were filling the earth, from the fighting of the war.

The climax came when he broke his sword in half, as Elvis bellowed out the remainder of the song's words, *His truth is marching on.*

Next was Lee Greenwood's voice that came across the speaker with "Proud to be An American" then the song "Georgia" filled the air, finishing up in a stirring climax. A person couldn't help but get teary eyed over such a wonderful nostalgic journey down memory lane, from the forgotten soldiers of the war to the present day of living in the United States of America.

The whole performance captivated one's heart and made one think back to the days of old and how far America has entered into the future. It made one think how a person was in deep gratitude to the forefathers and many others for everything they have endowed America with throughout one's journeys.

Mike, as well as Bonnie and their daughters, shed a few tears as the memories bounced with Lasers off the mountain carvings. Yes, one living in American could proudly say, *I'm glad to be in America...* The price of freedom was something that everybody should hold dearly, and never allow to slip through their fingers for any price.

When they returned to the room for a good night's rest, a cloudburst erupted as soon as they approached the door. As they got ready for bed, Mike occasionally looked out the door at the mountain. The rain descending from all around was another beautiful sight to behold. When it finally dissipated, you could see the steam arise from off the mountain top.

"Daddy," Michelle said, before retiring, "I'm really glad you brought us here. I loved the Laser Show the most. It made me do a lot of thinking. About then and now in our society."

"Yes, that it did" he answered, as he kissed her good night.

"I love you, Daddy. You're the best."

"Same goes for you kiddo. Better get some rest. Tomorrow we've got the Antique Auto and Music Museum—"

"And don't forget the Sky Lift," Michelle threw in, before he could finish.

"No, I haven't. But I think your mother would like to forget that long lift."

She giggled before running off to the bed.

Morning arrived. They ate breakfast at the Inn before heading to the Auto Show. It would be seen first, and then the Sky Lift.

Mike was absolutely enthralled with the Antique Auto and Music Museum, explaining to his family some of the things that they were observing that he had grown up with. It took more than the usual hour to view all the displays. He wanted to observe and take each of the items into his memory. Plus the girls were fascinated with the old jukeboxes, as well as Bonnie the five and ten cent movies. Especially the one titled, "Wife Catches Cheating Husband." Yes, she broke a dollar bill to get change to see that little number.

The next stop was the Sky Lift. Needless to say Bonnie was praying for rain. She didn't wish to go atop the high mountain area. With everyone aboard, they were off.

"Whew, look down at that scenery." Mike said to Bonnie.

She glanced once, and then turned the other way. The girls thought it funny. Heights didn't really bother them. Just before reaching the top, they saw the Sky Lift descending from the other side was making a plunge to the bottom.

"Boy that one was a little fast going down wasn't it?" he said to Bonnie, with raised eyebrows and a smile.

Her stomach felt squeamish. There was a slight rock before it straightened out. Mike and the girls found it a terrific jolt. Bonnie didn't.

Once atop of the mountain, others were walking around, some even going as far as the fence that bordered the edges. They walked as far as the little boxes, then placed a quarter inside to view the bottom area.

"Daddy," Victoria said. "I want to go down by the fence. How 'bout it?"

He cast Bonnie a glance then looked at all the others walking down that way. "I don't think so, sweetheart. You really might fall. And who's to say, knowing our luck at times, you might break through that fence barrier."

"Yeah, you're right."

They walked around a few more feet then circled some more area before boarding the Sky Lift to return them safely to the bottom.

Mike boarded and got right in front so that he could witness the view going down. "Hey, honey, wanna come stand in front with me?"

Bonnie looked down at the huge drop, and then rubbed her stomach. "No. I think I'll stand right behind you and hold onto these ropes. But thanks for the offer."

She watched, as again, Mike was having the time of his life. Often she would glance around to perhaps find John Candy or Chevy Chase nearby. She couldn't remove that adventure of Wally World from her mind, as she continued to view her husband's pleasure. She was glad that he was really enjoying himself.

Reaching the car and saying goodbye to the Sky Lift, they had one more stop before heading back to the room for a little relaxing. They wanted to cross over the old rustic covered bridge and visit the gristmill. The girls had a few more pictures they wanted to take.

They had enjoyed a light dinner at the new hotel not far away from where many of the golfers stayed. The girls thought it a very modern hotel, and wondered why they hadn't stayed in it. Then reconsidering the Inn where they were staying, they preferred it much better. At least from there they had a good view of the huge Stone Mountain.

The next morning brought sadness for each of them as they made preparations to check out and head for home. The trip had been so rewarding, they almost wished it could have lasted for more days but as with all things, it had to come to an end.

Viewing the scenery one last time, they tried to take in all the area's captivating beauty.

"Daddy, I wish we could live here, always," Michelle commented.

"Wouldn't that be heavenly? But I have to get back to work."

"I hope we can come back again next year, but stay longer," Victoria said.

"We'll see," Bonnie answered as they climbed in the car and said goodbye to all the wonderful sights and pleasures Stone Mountain had to offer.

On the way back home, they all talked about the wonderful events and times they had shared.

Mike glanced over to Bonnie. "Honey, I'm very glad we took this little trip."

"I am, too." She smiled while skimming through some of the booklets she had purchased.

"I still think we should at least consider moving up this way," Michelle mentioned.

"Honey, we have to go where Daddy can find work. And for now, he has a good paying job."

"Don't worry sunshine," he said, with a huge smile. "I'll bring all of you back next year. We'll stay longer than we did this round."

The girls, content with that answer, sat back and gazed out

the windows as the car rolled on down the highway.

"Honey," Bonnie said, looking up from the books, "According to this brochure, there's a lake right below the carving of the mountain."

"Yeah Mom, didn't you see it as we were riding in the Sky Lift?" Victoria inquired.

"No. Now, why didn't I see it?" Bonnie asked, disappointed.

"Probably because you were afraid to look down when the instructor on the tape was pointing out all the different spots surrounding the mountain area," Mike said, with a half grin.

"Yeah, guess so. But that really bothers me now. I can't believe I didn't get to view the lake."

"Well, Daddy, maybe we should turn around and take Mom back," Reneé said, with a laugh.

Looking at the back, through his rear view mirror, Mike chuckled as Bonnie joined in, along with the girls. Mike drove the Ford wagon down the interstate and Bonnie continued looking through the brochures.

Yeah, this was one trip he enjoyed. He couldn't wait to get home and tell the others, especially about the Laser Show. Thinking back to every song and part of that show, he would have to say that more than ever he was glad to be an American and living in the U.S.A. *Home Sweet Home.* Yes that was something that he proudly echoed in his mind. As he looked in the rearview mirror at his three daughters, then slowly allowed his eyes to rest on Bonnie for a moment, he knew he was indeed blessed to have such a grand place to live. Not only that, but a wonderful family to call his own in a journey that was getting better with each day.

The Vacationer
Bonnie's Fantasy

Bonnie glided across the room in an effort to get ready to meet her husband for a lunch engagement. They had taken another three-day vacation with their daughters, but today for lunch it would be just herself and her husband. There would likely be other faculty members already gathered in the dining room. To her it would be a nice luncheon without the constant nagging of the teenagers, or their stale, unnecessary jokes.

Bonnie looked at the time. It was almost ten. She hurriedly phoned room service. It would be a late breakfast, because they had overslept. With no impending housework, job or school to attend, each had taken the lazy mood and given in to being pampered with luxury. It had been a good while since they had last taken a trip away from home. She wanted to make the most of it.

When the breakfast arrived, she joined her daughters. Michelle switched on the television as they chowed down.

At home you could grab a piece of toast, cup of coffee and be on your way. This was different—the Inn's restaurant menu consisted of meals with full servings. Even a croissant and preserves ran higher than the store prices.

By the time the breakfast arrived it was already ten-thirty. They began distributing the food, arranging their plates in a buffet style. The food was indeed scrumptious, but half-way through the feast, the teenagers decided they were full and could eat no more.

"Oh, yes, positively, I'm stuffed," they agreed in unison, moaning in pain while rubbing the palms of their hands on their stomachs.

"You had such a different assortment of food that we had to try all of it," Victoria said.

Bonnie caught a glimpse of the food left on their plates. She looked at the time. It was slowly climbing to eleven o'clock. Maybe if she ate the tiny remainder it would be digested well before she joined her husband. She hated to see any food go to waste. She took a few bites. No, no more or she would be in the bathroom. She picked up the tray and placed it outside the door. Then she hastened to beautify herself for the man of her dreams.

Even though she was hurrying to get herself ready, she felt like a beautiful swan gliding across the hotel room as she applied her makeup. She looked twice in the mirror. Everything had to be just right.

"Mom, we are going to the fitness room to work off our breakfast," Michelle mentioned.

"What are you going to do about lunch, later? Go for the buffet or order room service?"

"Mother, please, let our breakfast stop swimming around first," Victoria said.

"I just want to be sure to tell your father that when the three of you get hungry, you will order something at your own discretion."

"Sure. Well, we've got our key," Reneé said. "Have fun with Daddy."

The door closed, leaving Bonnie to admire the view in the mirror. In a way she wished she were not leaving the room. The mere thought of having to order food was making her ill. She wished she could go to the fitness room and work off some of the pounds that no doubt were going to creep up after that huge breakfast.

Another glimpse at the clock. Oops, time to go. Mike would be sitting already at a table awaiting her entrance. Ready to leave, she tossed her hair to the side and readjusted the belt to her dress. She walked to the elevator, entered it, and pressed the button to the first floor. When she emerged from the elevator and approached the dining area, she noticed that her husband was already at a table with his plate full of food. He pulled the chair out for her, explaining how he only had forty minutes before the next class started, so he had to hurry and eat.

"You want to go ahead to the line, babe?" he asked with a smile. "Since it's a buffet, just help yourself. There is a huge selection."

"Would you be hurt if I only had a glass of water?" she asked, casually.

"Water? I thought we were having lunch together. Aren't you feeling well?"

"Honey, the girls and I, only a few minutes ago, finished breakfast. I sort of feel full."

The sad look that spread over his face was a bit too much. Forcing a smile, she got up and left to get a plate of food.

When she returned to the table, she suggested he stay seated; she could get her chair. He made no mention about her wee amount of food. "This roast beef is a bit too rare for my taste," he said.

"I like mine rare at times," she said, as she glanced over at his plate. His did look quite rare, reminding her of freshly cut meat. "Of course, I don't enjoy it that red."

"Where are the girls? I asked for a table for five."

Bonnie was somewhat taken aback. She had wondered why not a table for two. When she saw the other chairs she figured Mike had forgotten the plans.

"I thought this lunch was just for you and me. The girls said they wanted to stay to themselves today. After you heard their wish, you said it would be only the two of us."

He said nothing more on the matter. As she took dainty bites of her food, she wondered if he had really wanted the children to tag along. Couldn't they have one private time to be alone? He always wanted the children with them. She loved them just as much as him, if not more, but couldn't they once go somewhere without the girls? She had, after all, forgiven him of his indiscretion all those years ago. Even though their marriage was similar to a business marriage, she had at times missed the closeness that they shared when they first were married.

"I'm going to get some salad. Do you want some?" he asked, not really glancing at her when he spoke.

"No, I think this will be all I eat today."

She watched his form get up and stroll toward the buffet. The man was growing older but he was still in great shape. Sure, he wasn't the spring chicken he was when she first met him, but he still managed to take care of his body. Yet glancing at him this moment, she thought he seemed to be slowing down somewhat. She didn't know if it was from working so much or what. He always tried to stay busy. It often reminded her of her daddy and that bothered her. But what bothered her even more was the fact that Mike wouldn't open up and talk to her. To others he could express things better, but to his wife, after all these years—that was another subject in itself.

She took another bite of food, while she looked around at other tables, wondering what was being said, what others had ordered, and checking to see if she too was being watched by the oh, so careful eye. A vague notice again of Mike as he approached the table and took his seat. The only thing on his salad plate was fresh fruit. The man truly loved any variety of fruit that was in season.

She watched him as he ate a piece of cantaloupe.

Mike noticed her odd look. "What, was I suppose to bring you something?"

"No. I just can't get over it being only me and you at the table—alone."

"Yeah, it is sort of quiet. I am freezing though. Don't you think it is a wee bit cool in here?"

"No. In fact I had to turn the air up in the room before I left. The place was too stuffy and warm. Maybe you're getting a cold."

"Probably so."

She would occasionally cast an eye in his direction when he wasn't looking, observing his form as he ate with his elbows on the table.

Wicked sexy images began filling Bonnie's imaginative consciousness. The first to be one where she would lick her lips, wetting them moist with her tongue, as she playfully ran her foot up his pants leg. She could hear his instant reply.

"There are people here. What are you doing?"

But she would overlook his remark, casting it aside, and quickly push the dishes off the table onto the floor. Then she would climb atop, pulling him with her to the bare table. It would be there on the table that he would place his body under hers. She would give him the most excitable meal he had ever experienced in any restaurant.

There was a nudge of her husband's foot against her leg.

"Yes," she said with a cheeky smile.

"The waitress would like to know if you wish something other than water to drink."

Great going, she thought. There was no telling how long the woman had been standing over her, waiting for an answer while Bonnie fantasized about having sex with her husband in the middle of the Inn's most crowded restaurant.

Looking at the woman, Bonnie hoped her own face wasn't betraying her thoughts and blushing. "Sorry, my mind was elsewhere. Could I get a glass of unsweetened tea?"

Mike eyed his wife with concern as the petite waitress walked away from the table. "Are you all right today?"

"Of course I am. Why do you ask?"

"Since you came down from the room, it's like your mind has been in another dimension."

She wanted to admit that it had. First she had only wanted a glass of water, but no, there had to be a plate of food to join him for lunch, he hated eating alone. Then there was the query about the children joining them, thinking it was only going to be the two of them. That was followed by lack of communication on his part, allowing her mind to drift into passionate thoughts of them alone on this table, as she feasted on him as the main course.

"Sorry, you know how my mind is constantly active. I permitted it to become over clouded once more with all kinds of thoughts. Besides, I didn't exactly have your attention with you staring into your plate of food."

"Hon, I told you I only had a matter of minutes before I had to return to my class. I'm not feeling all that well, either."

She reached for his hand, fondly stroking it with hers. He did feel slightly chilled. The room itself was relatively warm—he was undoubtedly catching some bug.

Nothing more was said during the remainder of the meal. He said he would walk her back to the room. He needed a T-shirt under his shirt. Maybe that would keep him warmer.

After paying the guest check, she held his arm walking to the elevator. Another thought entered her mind as she boarded the small compartment, but she didn't elaborate on the fantasy. They only had four floors before reaching their room and even if she tried any moves on him, some people would be pushing the button that would allow the doors to open. Three of which could be their children. No, she would refrain from any ecstasy of a moment's pleasure in the tight receptacle of the elevator.

The tiny compartment came to a stop on the fourth floor. They got out and walked toward their room.

Again she walked arm in arm with him. Her hand slipped around his waist, edging its way down, silently making tracks on the back of his legs and buttocks.

"Bonnie, what are you doing?" he questioned, amazed that she would be making such moves on him in broad daylight.

"Oh, stop being such a fuddy-duddy. Look, I made sure no one was behind us. I'm only messing around. You know, being—*romantic.*"

She smiled, revealing a huge grin. He eyed her with raised eyebrows, and then continued strolling to the room.

There was a small corner next to the snack bar. Yank him in and go for the sweet nectar of his touch, his warmth. She envisioned all sorts of imaginative ways the two could be alone, enraptured in each others arms, locked by only fire and flame of the other's passion.

"Bonnie, what is with you today?"

"Mike, for once can't you be a little romantic?"

"That isn't in my vocabulary."

"Well, maybe it should be. You never want to be alone with me or anything. I love the girls too, but my goodness, don't you think we need some time to us alone?"

"We have always been together."

"There's a time when we need to be alone, just you and me."

"Bonnie, you knew I wasn't all that romantic when we married."

"I thought as you grew older you might possibly change. And you were somewhat more romantic before you started all your little endeavors. Oh, never mind. I don't want to bring up the past. That is dead and gone."

"Look, I'm sorry that I can't make you happy anymore. I need to get another shirt and get back to class."

Bonnie stood still as Mike walked off. Her thoughts roamed. Mike was one person she was really finding hard to understand anymore.

"Mom...oh, Mom."

Standing at the door's entrance, Bonnie awoke from her daze. Michelle stood in front of her.

"Mom, are you okay?"

"Yes. I was just doing a little daydreaming."

"Daddy went in to get another shirt. He said he wasn't feeling well. I hope he's not getting a bug. You look a little pale yourself. Maybe you should come in and take a little nap."

"Maybe I will."

Reneé took hold of her mother's arm and escorted her to the room. The rest of the days would be filled with more fun with all family members, and less on fantasy and so much menu planning. Even if it meant only a glass of water for her, that would be all she would be ordering. She didn't know if it was the fullness of the meals or what. Mike's behavior was bothering her as well. Couldn't he see that she needed him? Over the years she had forgiven him for his indiscretion. She really had. He had promised that when the girls were grown it would be just the two of them. When was that time ever going to arrive?

"Bonnie, got to go back to the meeting. Look, I'm sorry. We'll spend some time together later, I promise."

She watched as he walked down the hallway. There was something happening to Mike. She didn't know what it was but she was sure the outcome wasn't going to be good. This was one trip she wasn't going to forget. The trip they had to Stone Mountain was much better than this one.

A Refreshment Most Rewarding
Another Calm Before the Storm

Bonnie took her husband's handkerchief and blotted sweat from her forehead. For June, it was immensely hot, almost like a furnace in this part of the country. Just glancing at the empty wasteland made it appear like hot steam was surfacing from the pavement. She looked up and down the long stretch of highway. There was no sign of any cars, not even a bug crossing the hot steamy highway. To the side of the road there were no billboards, only a few telephone poles scattered along the parched, barren land. Too bad she couldn't climb atop one of the poles and tap into someone's line, then maybe she and Mike could get a tow truck out this way.

"Bonnie, are you going to give me a hand, or stand and look at the scenery all day?" Mike growled from under the car hood.

"Mike, I am not looking at the scenery, as you so hatefully pointed out. I'm looking to see if any cars are coming by. If there was any way we could climb up on the telephone pole, we could tap into someone's line for help."

Mike turned his head away from the car engine and glanced toward the spot where she was standing. "Bonnie, I thought when I married you, you had brains. Did the steamy heat erase all of your knowledge?"

"Funny, ha, ha."

"Besides, if a car were to happen to come by, I can assure you we would definitely see it. As for climbing one of those telephone poles, I think the hot sun has really gotten to you."

"Well at least I would know to get a car that wasn't going to give us any trouble. I told you to get a Ford."

"Look, Bonnie, American cars break down once in a while too, or have you forgotten the last Ford wagon we had?"

"No, but I told you to check this one out before you decided to drive from Georgia to Arizona."

"I had it serviced. Your information data file must have misplaced that section."

"Is that supposed to be funny or taken as sarcasm?"

"Bonnie, I don't want to fight. The heat is too fiery to be starting any argument. It is causing enough conflict for us now. You wanted a vacation—just the two of us, remember? I don't think we need to be spatting over this. Is there any water left in the carrier?"

She walked over to the car and looked in the back seat. Pulling out the small blue canister, she unscrewed the lid and looked inside.

"Half full. Do you need it for the radiator?"

"No," he remarked, slamming the car's hood, then wiping the sweat from his forehead.

"Oh, got it fixed?"

"No, I don't got it fixed," he barked. "I need the water. I'm going to start walking until I find a gas station with a tow truck. Do you want to come with me or stay here? We have to do something. The cell phone doesn't even work out here in these flatlands."

"How many miles do you think we will have to walk before we get to one?"

Once again he rubbed the sweat off his forehead with his soiled hand. "I wish I could see how far this highway goes, but unfortunately that is impossible."

"You don't have to get so hostile. I just thought you might have an estimate."

"Well, I'm sorry, Your Grace, but I don't. Are you coming or not? If you are, then lock up the car and come on."

She shot him a cold stare.

"What now?" He fumed.

"Your fuse is a little too short for me. I'm going, but I'm walking behind. I don't think I wish to get close to your dynamite stack at this moment. You know when the girls are with us you don't act like this. Are you afraid to be alone with me or what?"

"I don't know what you are talking about."

"Face it, Mike. You never want to be alone with me. Even on this trip. You were hesitant, hoping that I would change my mind and invite the girls. They do have their own lives now. I'll ask you again, are you afraid of me?"

"Ha, ha," he said, turning and walking off toward the sun's direction.

Bonnie grabbed her tiny tape recorder, the water canister, locked the doors, and then followed Mike.

"I hope you left those windows rolled down a little, so they won't crack," he called over his shoulder.

"Give me some credit," she threw back.

Mike resented more than anything being intimated by his wife. *Afraid of her?* A lot of people wanted to bring their children along on vacation. What was wrong with that? Then again he had promised they would have their time when the girls got older. Why couldn't he just tell her that he hadn't been feeling well lately? He had mentioned it to her on previous occasions. No, no sense in bringing it up again. She would start worrying. He didn't want that. He was sure the constant bickering wasn't helping either one of them. He would have to tell her soon or try to change. He would probably go for the latter.

Occasionally he would look toward his rear and watch as she steadily took another step in the fierce heat. *That dad-blamed tape recorder,* he said under his breath. Constantly she had to have it with her no matter where they were. Ever since she chose to work in a library, she carried it around to come up with traveler's stories to tell everyone that she saw at her book club. No doubt she would have a fabulous story to tell about this trip. He could hear it now.

"Husband heads out to Arizona in a foreign car, mind you. As he enters Arizona, on his way to the Grand Canyon, the car breaks down. They have to walk for hundreds of miles to find a gas station." Yeah, she would paint him as the ugliest villain in the west.

As Bonnie trudged along behind Mike, her thoughts were not on the car breaking down, but rather on dipping herself in a nice cold pool of water. She wanted to keep her mind busy so the tiredness that she was already beginning to feel, in her feet and legs, would not control her system. No way would she tell Mike that she couldn't keep up with him. That would only cause another argument.

"Should have worked out more, I tried to tell you."

He never did much exercise anymore but whenever she fell behind and missed one day, he would throw in how she had missed a day. Her first mistake had been to tell him, "Don't ever let me miss a day without a walk or my daily regimen." She didn't wish to have that thrown in her face again.

Yeah, I see you every once in a while looking in my direction, Bonnie said under her breath. *You are probably wondering if I can keep up with you. Well, we will just wait and see won't we, Mike Fairmont. Besides I have the canister of water.* She giggled to herself.

Now that was a vision for her book club classmates. She turned on the tiny tape recorder and began feeding it full of information.

"Funny how water has been here since the beginning of creation and I can't even locate a lake, river, or even a stream to cool myself with that wonderful refreshing, sparkling clear liquid. As I walk along this barren dry land I wonder how it would be living out here with no faucet to turn on to brush my teeth, wash my hair, take a bath, or even dive into at this moment to cool my hot, sweaty body.

"Believe me I am perspiring like a hog, to use an old expression. A person doesn't know how lucky they are to be in their homes at this moment. As I walk along this wasteland following the Green Giant or should I say the Incredible Green Hulk at this time, I am reminded of our earlier forefathers. Their task of drawing water was not easy compared to the pleasure we have in receiving it nowadays. They couldn't turn on a knob or push a button at a water fountain and bingo, have instant water.

"Amazing though, how they still found ways to retrieve water for drinking, cooking and practical use. I imagine a lot of you young girls would squirm to have to carry the drinking water from the lakes and stream's of God's beautiful land to your warrior or family. I can almost hear the sounds as I walk now. Who me? No, my back is not strong enough to carry such a heavy barrel.

"Sorry, young ladies, back then you couldn't get away with stuff like you do now. If you boys think it's funny, there isn't anything to laugh about. You, too, would be in a burdensome boat. I think when I get back, if I live to get back, this mountain man up ahead of me may strike me dead before we reach a gas station; but if I get back we will have a very interesting discussion. Okay, enough ranting now. Let me shut this off. This heat is unbearable."

She inhaled what breath of air she could. If only it would rain then it would cool their hot, sticky bodies. How long had they been walking? It seemed like for ages. No matter how she tried to steer her mind to another subject, the scorching heat of the cracked road was hot to the bottom of her Reeboks. They may have been walking shoes, but in this extreme heat it didn't help. She wondered if Mike was feeling the road's heat under his feet. Even if he did he would probably keep silent on the matter. He hated confessing anything to her.

Mike eyed a medium size boulder with a short tree towering over it. He perched himself against the hard rock. He watched as Bonnie approached, staggering to keep up. Yeah, she was putting on a good act for him. He knew she had to be in torment. One thing was for sure, he was wishing he were in the ocean with all the fish. At least he would be moderately chilled in the cool water. He croaked a giggle.

"Something amusing? Perhaps me trying to catch up to you?" she questioned, as she neared his side.

"No. I was just wishing I was a fish in the sea."

"One thing is for sure, we would be refreshed."

"Come here woman, this smelly man wants to give you a sweaty hug."

"Sure you wouldn't rather strike me because of all my outbursts?"

"Maybe later. For now I just want to put my manly arms around your body."

She enveloped him in her arms as he hugged her tightly.

"I love you, Bonnie. Always remember that."

"The feeling is mutual."

"So what bad things were you saying about me on the recorder this time?" he inquired.

"Nothing. I was preparing a class for my book students on the importance of water and how necessary it is for us. Too many take its use for granted until they are desperately in need of it. I thought that would make a good discussion in our book club."

"Isn't that the truth? If we ever make it back home, I know I will consider more of its use when I turn on the faucet for drinking or bathing, even washing that red Mazda down the road. Wanna give me some now before we go any farther?"

She handed him the canister. When he finished he gave it back to her.

"That takes care of our water supply," she said, finishing off the water. "Honey, next time we decide to take a vacation, let's go to Venice; at least there we will be surrounded by the blessed water."

"You bet, sweetheart. Bonnie, I'm sorry I've been such a heel. I will try to be better. Guess some things I am still set in my ways. Do you forgive me?"

"I can't stay mad at you, Mike. I love you too much."

"I think I spot a gas station up a ways. Why don't we make tracks and check it out?"

Bonnie glanced toward the highway that lay ahead.

"Are you sure it isn't a mirage?" she questioned.

"This, I am sure of. I say we make haste."

"Why, so he doesn't close before we can get a tow truck?"

"Who's talking tow trucks? I want some more of that sparkling water."

"Wanna race?" she asked, running off ahead of him.

Mike laughed as he raced toward Bonnie. He would try to make this a happy trip for her. He didn't want her to know how he was really feeling. Maybe in time these spells would go away. At least he hoped so. For now he felt as if his journey of late was slowing to a steadier pace. He thought of his dear mother and how her sickness had started to threaten her appearance when she grew ill. He really hoped in his heart that it was just a passing bug. One thing he didn't wish was to leave Bonnie and his three beautiful daughters.

The Heartbreak
Shadows of Gloom Come Knocking

As Mike looked back on his journey through the years, there had been sad times as well as happy ones. The girls had brought so much joy to their lives. He and Bonnie had been so blessed to have them. Years had turned them into beautiful young women. Victoria and Reneé had finished school and some college, then married. Reneé had already given birth to a baby boy. This had thrilled Mike. He loved little girls but after having raised three, he was looking forward to this little grandson. Even when they announced it would be a boy, Bonnie insisted it would be a girl. She wanted a granddaughter. That way she could dress her in little outfits or style her hair. When they rolled mother and son out and Bonnie saw the little bundle, it didn't matter. Mother and son were both fine. The little boy was a wonderful addition to their family.

Not long after that, Michelle decided that she was in love. She started skipping school. Mike was extremely hurt when he heard the news. She and Tommy were in love. They wanted to marry.

"Michelle, you are only seventeen. You have one year of school left."

"Daddy, Tommy and I can't wait. We want to get married now."

"Are you pregnant?"

"NO!"

"Then why the rush?"

"We want to be together. If you don't sign for us, we will just live together."

"Not under my roof."

"You can't stop us."

"Where is all this coming from young lady? You act as if you are a grown-up and pay rent around here. Oh, let me think back. If I'm not mistaken you wanted to move out when you were thirteen. Yeah, you called up one of your little friends and asked, could you move in with them? It almost gave me a heart attack. Then you informed me when you turned seventeen that *you* could do whatever you wanted too. Your little friends had told you that. Honey, your little friends aren't always right."

"So what are you going to do? Arrest me? Lock me up in my room?"

"I could start with Tommy."

Bonnie tried to calm matters. "Michelle, please, don't upset your dad. You know that he hasn't been well."

"Like she cares, Bonnie. She has hurt me so many times over the years that I doubt if I will ever heal inside." Mike glared at Bonnie.

"And you have never hurt me, Daddy?"

"Oh, because I didn't let you go out all hours of the night or walk up and down the streets with your little friends, I have hurt you? I have only protected you, Michelle. There is nothing that I wouldn't do for any of my daughters."

Bonnie knew that was true. He had made the remark

once that he always loved his children more than anything or anyone. Even though it was during their distance, he had never once corrected it to Bonnie. It was something she would go to her grave remembering.

"Then allow me to marry Tommy."

"After you have finished school and gotten a good job young lady. Let me ask you something. How is he going to support you?"

"He is getting a job with his dad."

"What about school?"

"He is dropping out."

"Dropping out? Did you hear that Bonnie? They both are dropping out. Now you tell me what kind of good paying job that a dropout is going to find? They have no place to live, yet they are going to have a job."

"Michelle, I have to agree with your Dad. You need to finish school first. You only have one year to go."

"I want to live with Tommy. I'm not happy here. You and Daddy don't even have a marriage."

"Why, because we aren't like the Brady Bunch family? Wake up, Michelle, that is television," Mike interjected.

"Michelle, please, I don't think you realize how you are upsetting your dad. Both of you need to calm down. Nothing will ever get resolved from all this bickering."

"If you don't sign then we are moving in with Tommy's parents."

Bonnie was afraid that Mike would floor Michelle right then.

"Why don't you just get a knife and stab me in the heart, Michelle. Just let me end my life now."

"Mike, please," Bonnie pleaded.

"If you move in with those people you are no longer my daughter."

"Mike, you don't mean that," Bonnie pleaded.

"Just try me, Bonnie. She is no longer my daughter if she chooses that life. You know she hasn't been herself since she turned thirteen. Don't start standing up for her now. When I overheard her ask Mrs. Sizemore, could she move in with them, that killed me. No one will ever know what I went through over that little episode."

"I was there, Mike. It hurt me, too. Or have you forgotten? We need to think about the present now. None of us need to put barriers in our paths right now. You two are headed for a full scale war." Bonnie rubbed her forehead. "Look, Michelle, you can't move in with Tommy."

"Then sign for me to marry. Grandmother said you should do this."

Mike sent a stare straight to Bonnie.

"Don't look at me. I didn't know anything about this," Bonnie replied.

"I am your father, Michelle. As long as you live under my roof, you will do as I say until you are grown."

"I love Tommy, Daddy. Please accept that."

"You are my baby girl, my sweet pea. I will never accept you wasting your life this way. Tell me something and be honest. The days that you were skipping school were you sleeping with him? Did you bring him into our home?" Mike asked, then crossed his arms.

Michelle eyed Bonnie.

"Michelle, don't tell me..." Mike didn't finish. He ran over and took hold of Michelle's neck.

"Mike, stop it! Have you gone crazy?" Bonnie pulled him

away.

Mike broke into tears. "Get your stuff and get out of here! NOW! Call that man up and have him park at the end of the driveway. He is never to come in this yard again. Do you hear me? I will never forget this Michelle. You have really disappointed me. All I did was love you and care for you. That is what a parent does. You will understand one day if you are lucky to have any children of your own."

Michelle cried when he left the room. She made her call, then Bonnie watched as she gathered some items.

"Michelle, really think about this. Your daddy loves you so much. I love you. He only wants the best for you. It was hard on him when Victoria and Reneé moved out and married."

"It was hard on me, too. Tell me, Mother, why have you stayed with him all these years? For the sake of the children? What about your happiness?"

"Michelle, I pity you. You don't understand anything about devotion and commitment. But you will, as you grow older. It's a shame that young people don't understand that until later in life. Or maybe they are too involved in fun things that they don't care to understand the real meaning of love. You don't stay with someone for twenty-five years and feel nothing for the other person. Sure, I've been hurt. Who hasn't in this world? That comes with the package. I know it has brought distance but it has brought feelings that I can't explain either."

Bonnie paused and ran a finger over her forehead as she inhaled a deep breath.

"Sure, you girls were a big part of my decision to stay all these years, but it was my decision. It didn't hurt you girls. I would do it all again so you would grow up with a mother and father together. I have mentioned the same to your sisters. Marriage is more than just saying you love someone. It's a lifelong commitment. A job that you have to work on daily. You can't just throw in the towel when something goes wrong. Marriage vows are important to me. I really hope when you get older that you will realize this. Your father is a good man. He has always supported us and been there for us. The good times have always outweighed any bad ones. Life and marriage is more than sex, Michelle."

Tears fell down Michelle's cheeks. She looked out the window.

"Tommy is out there. I better go."

"You could always change your mind."

"So could Daddy."

They embraced before Michelle went out the door.

Mike sat on the back porch. He lit one cigarette after another. He waited until he heard the car drive off before going inside the house.

"You are probably going to tell me that I should sign."

"Mike, I wasn't going to say anything. But if they are so much in love, maybe we should go ahead and sign. Everyone has to learn and live through their own mistakes."

"They don't have jobs, Bonnie. They are dropping out of school. My baby is just throwing her future down the drain. What do you want us to do, allow them to move in here and support them?" His words mingled with tears.

"It would be better then her moving in with his parents. You know how they are. I'm sure that they can find jobs, Mike."

"I'm going out to smoke."

Bonnie stared at him. "What? Haven't you had enough? You smell like you've been putting out a fire."

"Bonnie, I'm in no mood for nagging," he said, then stormed out the door.

The weeks ahead weren't easy for Mike or Bonnie. They seldom spoke. The days for Mike consisted of getting up, going to work, coming home, eating, then smoking a cigarette, then off to bed. Bonnie was worried. Mike's health wasn't as good as it used to be.

By the end of the month he had agreed to sign for Michelle to marry. He was tired of fighting. He had a grandson to think about. He didn't want to have an early death.

The months ahead Bonnie and Mike still remained distant. She wondered, would they ever become close again? The girls were all married now, if she wanted to leave Mike, there were no small children any longer. But she loved him, even though he was driving her away again, she loved him more than ever. They never had relations any more. All Mike wanted to do was sit outside and smoke.

One day it was too much for him. He was being admitted into the hospital for angioplasty. Unfortunately it turned into a heart attack on the table. Bonnie lost it when the doctor came out to tell her. They would have to do emergency surgery. It was something that she hadn't anticipated.

She remembered hugging him as they hurried him into the operating room. The nurse was having trouble removing his wedding band. She remembered hearing someone say they would have to cut it off, then the doctor instructing her to run it under soapy, warm water. They wouldn't be cutting any wedding band off. It was chaos.

Bonnie phoned the girls and her mother. They would be

down soon. She went into the hospital chapel to pray. It was a prayer that she would never forget. By the time the others reached the hospital, Mike was already in surgery.

Bonnie's mother comforted her daughter. The girls, as well as their husbands, expressed concern. The surgery started at nine-thirty in the morning. It was after five o'clock before the doctor came out of the room. Bonnie would remember that Labor Day weekend the rest of her life. Dr. Wilson had been very concerned. Mike had to have a quadruple bypass. They had to cut a vein from his right leg, from the top of the thigh to his ankle to replace his bad arteries. The doctor had sat with him for two hours and watched over him to make sure he was all right. He advised Bonnie that everything should be okay, but Mike needed to stop smoking. His arteries had been bad, very bad. The next time he might not be that lucky. He would be in intensive care for a good while.

Bonnie and her mother were the first to go in to see him. They were only permitted a small amount of time. Bonnie shed silent tears. She hadn't seen so many tubes and wires running through anyone's body. He looked so helpless. His breathing was erratic.

"Don't worry," the nurse said. "It's the machine. It's helping his breathing now. We have to keep an eye on his weight, too, and make sure no fluid fills his lungs."

The others were allowed a few minutes to see their dad. It was unbelievably hard on everyone—more so on Michelle. Bonnie stayed until the nurse suggested she go home and rest. There was no need staying in the hospital. She would be no good to Mike without rest herself. It was extremely difficult to leave him, but they assured her that he was in capable hands. He would be monitored every minute of the night. If anything were to happen she would be notified. Bonnie touched his hand then kissed his forehead before leaving. She cried all the way home.

The next morning she phoned Bryan. He would be leaving Panama City soon. He would drive up to see his brother. None of the others could make it. Bonnie didn't expect anyone else. Bryan had been the only one who had really stayed in contact.

She went to the hospital alone. The others would be by later. It was early. She had to see Mike. When she entered the room she noticed he was receiving blood.

"It's okay," the nurse stated. "His blood count is way down. The doctor ordered it."

"How much are you going to have to give him?"

"We are hoping just this one unit."

Mike blinked his eyes and looked over to Bonnie. The tube was still in his mouth and nose.

"He started coming around a few minutes ago. He's been doing a little talking, too."

"How much longer is he going to continue to be on this breathing machine?"

"The doctor is hoping to remove it by the end of the day. If not then, probably by morning. I'll leave the two of you alone."

Bonnie brushed Mike's hair from his forehead. "Hi, honey. I'm glad to see you awake. You gave us all a bit of a scare."

"The girls?" he whispered.

"They will be here soon. It is still early." Tears began misting in her eyes. "I'm sorry. I didn't mean to do this in front of you. I'm trying to be strong."

"It's okay," he said in a soft whisper.

"I knew those cigarettes would eventually do this to you."

"Don't. Not a word."

Bonnie bit her tongue. It wasn't the time or the place. She was just so upset with the whole ordeal. She wished she had a camera to take pictures of his condition to show him later. He had pushed himself too far with all his bad habits. Didn't he realize what this was doing to her and the children? He slowly stretched out his hand.

"It will be all right," he said, softly. "I hurt. These tubes hurt."

Yeah, and if you could have a cigarette you would probably light one up right now, Bonnie thought.

"Honey, I spoke to Bryan again this morning. He was getting ready to get on the road. If the traffic wasn't too heavy, he said he should be here around one."

Mike stared off at the wall. Bonnie didn't know what to say. He was like a caged animal, unable to move.

"Mike, would you like for me to leave?"

"No, sit by me." He was in so much pain. He didn't want her to have to see him in this shape but he didn't want to be alone either.

She sat by his side until the girls showed up. Every once in awhile she could see a tear escape from his eye.

Bryan arrived around two. The traffic flow had been heavy.

"Bryan, he's miserable. I can't do anything to help him. Not only that, he is back to pushing me away again," Bonnie said.

Bryan embraced her. "I'm sorry you're having to go through this."

"How long can you stay?"

"I can only stay the night, kiddo. I've got a huge case we are working on."

"Guess the police force keeps you pretty busy?"

"As always."

Bonnie opened the door to the room. "Girls, Uncle Bryan is here."

They gave him a hug. It was good to get to see him again. Bonnie and the girls went to the waiting room to leave the brothers alone.

It was a touching reunion for the two. Tears filled Mike's eyes. Bryan told him that he couldn't have any of that. They would throw him out. But Bryan shed a few tears himself. It was good to get to see his brother even if it was under sad circumstances. Of all the family they were the only ones who had stayed in close contact. They were happy for that.

The next day Bryan headed back to Florida. Mike was taken off the breathing machine. In time the tubes and wires were removed as well. A wound from a piece of tape had left a mark on his arm.

"Sorry about that," the orderly replied. "We had to hold the tube in place."

Bonnie thought the man had been a little rough with Mike. She wondered if he was a new student. She would be glad when Mike was out of the hospital and back home with her. She would make sure he was taken care of. After five days they moved him into PCU. They wanted to monitor him a couple more days before releasing him to a regular room.

Mike was restless. He wanted out. He wanted a cigarette. Everyday, a male nurse had to come in and beat on his back to loosen a little phlegm. He had to cough it all up. Everything had to be expelled from his chest and lungs if he wanted to get out and go home.

"Come on, Mr. Fairmont. You've got to cough it up. Hold this little pillow tightly to your chest. That will help some of the pain. I know it hurts but you have to do it. I'll let them bring your little grandson to the edge of the door. Would you like that?"

Mike fought back tears. "Yes."

A few minutes later Bonnie brought little Robert to the edge of the door.

"Robert, there is Grandpa."

He reached for his grandpa. "No, sweetie, Grandpa can't hold you yet. He has to get well first."

Robert clapped his little hands. Mike burst into tears.

"Hi, baby. How's my little grandbaby? Grandpa loves you."

"Pa, pa."

"We've got to go outside now. Say bye to Grandpa. He has to get some rest."

He waved his little hand. "Bye, pa, pa."

Mike wiped his tears when Bonnie went out. When she returned he was staring out the window.

"Mike, I hope that wasn't too much on you. I know how you insisted on seeing him."

"No. I needed to see the little fella. Bonnie, I need to get out of here. I'm getting edgy."

"Probably the lack of nicotine, too."

"I wondered when you would start in."

"The doctor is concerned. He said you couldn't start back to your old habits. You have to watch your diet, too."

"So you are going to start nagging?"

"No. But I am not going through this again. This is painful on your family, too. There is going to be therapy for a month when they release you. The doctor said that you would be out of work for three months. He said he might let you return in six weeks if you are doing the minimum of duties."

"How will we pay the bills?"

"Everything is going to be fine. You don't need to be worrying about anything."

"I am the head of the household. How am I supposed to feel?"

"The same way if it were me in your place and you were caring for me. Stop being macho for once."

Mike reached for her hand and patted it. He knew they had a long road ahead of them.

* * * *

Mike was finally released. Bonnie had to help him shower and get about for a good four weeks. By the time she took him to the doctor, then therapy and cared for him, not to mention her job, she was exhausted. She would cry so many nights without him seeing her. The first time he needed help in the shower, the tears just poured. It was the first time she had actually looked at the staples in his body. They ran all down the front of his chest and along the right top of the leg to the ankle. It had all been too much on her.

They had to view tapes about the after effects of the operation. Not only was it difficult on the patient but on the spouse as well. It was something they both would have to adjust to. Mike found himself breaking down and crying over the smallest things, even a sentimental movie would get to him. Then after thirty-two days of therapy he started back smoking.

"Look, Mike, if you are going to start back smoking, just go ahead. As for hiding it, I can smell it on you. I'm not going to nag you. I just want you to know I can't put myself through this again. Maybe you enjoyed going through all of that but it was no hayride for me."

"Bonnie, I have smoked since I was a very young boy. It's hard to stop. I won't smoke as much. I promise that I will only eat the healthy foods that you prepare for me."

She chose not to argue. She was too exhausted for that.

In time he continued to improve. After three months he was able to return to work as before, the only difference being no strenuous heavy lifting or riding any fast roller coasters or anything like that anymore. He had to learn to adapt to a whole new lifestyle. Even intimacy was frightening to him. He kept telling the doctor that he wasn't ready. He was afraid that he might have a heart attack. The doctor assured him that was all in his head. Bonnie said that she understood and never pressured him.

As the days ran into months then years, Reneé had given birth to another baby boy. Michelle and Tommy started having troubles. She went as far as taking an overdose of pills hoping that it would bring Tommy to his senses. The only thing it did was worry Mike and Bonnie. After some counseling, they were able to help Michelle and Tommy overcome their obstacles. A year later Michelle gave birth to a beautiful baby boy.

Everything seemed to be going pretty well for Mike. He thought of his family often. When brother Robert had to have open-heart surgery, he and Bryan flew to Ohio to be with him. They were able to get the other brothers together, too. It had been a reunion that Mike was grateful to attend. Still there had been no word of sister. No one knew of her whereabouts. Even with Bryan being with the police force, he had not been able to locate her.

Bonnie's life seemed to be settling. She and Mike had become close companions. That was important at their age. The best event came when, after six years of marriage, Victoria finally gave birth to her first child, a baby boy. She didn't care what it was as long as it was healthy. She was just overwhelmed to be blessed to have a child like her sisters.

This was a journey in Mike's life that he was extremely happy with. He wanted the best for all his girls, but as always there was something about Victoria. He had missed so much of her first year of life when he had been away at war. Now that she had her own little bundle of joy everything just seemed to fall into place.

He looked through the old photographs. So many things had changed. It had been nine years since his first quadruple bypass. Now he was getting over radiation and chemo treatments. Nine years later, he had suffered a small heart attack and had to be admitted into the hospital once again. This time it was open-heart surgery again on the same area where they had operated nine years ago. He had never stopped smoking. He had tried but the addiction was too strong for him.

After he had the heart attack in March, the doctor told him that he needed to see about having his lungs checked out. He would have to get with another doctor about that. When Mike was released from the hospital he had to be put on oxygen for three weeks. When his breathing finally cleared up, the oxygen was removed. He was told that he would have to go at a steady pace and would not be able to work again. This had hit him hard. All he had done in his life was work and take care of his family. Why was this being taken from him? He tried to accept it but it wasn't an easy thing to swallow.

There was so much to do around the house and he just wasn't able to do much of anything anymore. The sons-in-law came over to help when they had time, but Mike found himself more edgy. Things needed to be done, and he would have to be the one to do them, to get them done no matter how many times Bonnie insisted he wasn't capable. Didn't she understand? Being a man, you didn't stop working no matter how bad off you were? He knew she was only trying to help him stay well and live longer, but she didn't understand what this did to a man.

By December he decided to climb a ladder and cut down some tree limbs. Thirty minutes later he was in the emergency room with a wrist broken in several places, and a collarbone that had to be set. For six weeks, Mike had to endure pins and needles in his arm and wrist. It was a time that he would never forget. Bonnie said it once, and she said she would never say, *I told you so* again. She had been so hurt by the ordeal. Mike was getting unbearable to be around when it came to her. She couldn't do right and Mike was always telling the children, Daddy loves you and giving *them* hugs. With Bonnie it was something different, and this hurt her more than he could imagine. It was taking too much of a toll on her as well. But for some reason, Mike couldn't see that.

Only one good thing had come out of the fall from the ladder. The x-ray had shown a spot on his lung that proved to be cancerous. Mike shed a tear when the doctor told him that the cancer was terminal. The tumor was so advanced in his lung that his breathing was being hampered. Fortunately weeks of chemo and radiation shrunk the tumor in his lung but other cancers had been spotted in his liver area.

Mike leaned back in the chair and looked out over the yard as he lit another cigarette. He was told to stop, but anymore that was all that he felt he had to give him any enjoyment. He was terminal. They had no idea how many days or even years he had left on his journey. The addiction would not go away. It might for other people but it didn't for him. He was even told his contact with Agent Orange when he was overseas was responsible for most of his cancer.

Of late, he had been having recurring nightmares of the war. He didn't understand why. All that was in the past. He never even thought of it anymore. Yet the nightmares were growing worse. He even had to see a psychiatrist for his nightmares. Another thing that was bothering him was Bonnie. He knew, in his heart, that he was shoving her away but something was happening to his body. He couldn't be the man that he once was. All he knew was in time he would die. He would no longer be able to see his grandsons, his lovely daughters or his wife again. Soon his journey would be over. His cards had been cut.

He eyed the cigarette one last time before he put it out and went inside the house. All he did anymore was sit and watch the news or go outside for a cigarette when the urge struck him. He kept the house very warm because he was always freezing. He had gone from a man of one hundred eighty-five pounds to a man of one hundred forty-one pounds so fast. He hated the fact that he was losing his hair, but then again the chemo had shrunk some of the tumor. He was most thankful to his Maker for that.

He kept in touch with the children. He broke into tears very easily. They had tried to accept it, but it was equally hard on them as well. And he hated more than anything to be alone. He had pushed Bonnie away so many times that he couldn't blame her when she went to visit places that he didn't want to go. He had turned into a harsh man in his last days. He never understood if it was because he knew being terminal he didn't have many days left, or because he was bitter with what the war had brought on him as well as the cigarettes that had been a poison to his body.

He stood in the living room viewing all the portraits that hung on the wall. He pulled the robe tighter around his body trying to feel its warmth. The pain was so unbearable at times. They had prescribed painkillers and sleeping aids, but they only worked for so long before they lost their effect. His thoughts turned to his mother, then his father who had died not many years after his first heart surgery. He had only been able to see him four times since his mother's passing. He thought of his baby sister that he had never seen since their mother's death. He thought of so many things that had revolved around him. Some good, some bad. He would have to say that he had been a most lucky man for living the years that he had thus far. In his mind he had kept a mental diary of everything that had transpired in his life. Events including his dear wife and family.

He eyed the notebook on the coffee table that Victoria and her husband had given him. Inside were stories that he had told them, snapshots that had been taken of him and his loving family and the grandchildren. Moments that couldn't be wiped out by anyone. Ones that were planted in his heart to be cherished and treasured forever until the end of time.

His mind swam back to events with his dear mother. He remembered her loving kindness and how she had brought six sons into the world, then a daughter. Now his daughters all had sons. He had three beautiful daughters, three wonderful sons-in-law, four great grandsons, and the best wife in the world. Even if he never was able to see his only sister in this life again, he felt blessed. As Mike Fairmont pondered on his journeys he knew he had a complete family. Not only was he a happy man, he was indeed truly blessed.

The journey from a boy to a man had not been an easy one. There had been some obstacles that were harder than others, yet he had managed to live some good days with people that he loved dearly. Not many people even got to live as many years as he had. And not many got to have such a loving family as he had. Life was too short for anyone born into this world. One should make it the best life has to offer. As for Mike Fairmont, even with the disease that was now dwelling inside his body, he knew, in his heart, that his journeys from a boy to a man were something that he had enjoyed everyday of his life.

AUTHOR'S NOTE

These stories are very special to me and my daughters. Bob would tell us so many stories about his life when he was growing up and he would share many stories with his sons-in-law when he was in the war. Tommy was always fascinated with the one where Bob was in the foxhole and had to take the initiative to jump out of the foxhole and take the weapon to save his men. For this he was honored with the Medal of Valor. It always pained him to have to see so many lives go off to war, but being in the military he knew it was his duty to not only protect his family but his country. He was a great provider and a loving husband, father and grandfather, and we truly miss him. Life is just not the same without him.

The stories that he told us we made into stories of another man taking a journey similar to his.

I am grateful to Debra Womack, Marsha Briscoe and Whiskey Creek Press for making his dream come true. He didn't live to see the book in print, but he knew about it.

ABOUT THE AUTHOR

Linda Lattimer lives in southern Georgia. Writing is a passion she enjoys. Writing allows her a sense of escape. Books take you places you can only read about and you meet people who stay in your heart forever. Linda enjoys traveling and seeing new places. *Raymond Gary Park,* in Oklahoma, is a place she frequents because of the beauty and serenity it offers. Her other published books include *Ready, Willing and...Abel;* an anthology, *Brides and Bouquets;* and *Skeletons Too Close To Home.* Take a look at her website for all the books she currently has out, and the new releases to come.

To learn more about Linda, visit her website: http://www.coffeetimeromance.com/OurAuthors/LindaLLattimer/AboutMe.html

*For your reading pleasure, we in-
vite you to visit our web bookstore*

WHISKEY CREEK PRESS

www.whiskeycreekpress.com